DANCE OF THE MASKS

Rue Morgan loved earning her living as a market gardener and was shattered when she learned that she was to lose both her home and livelihood. But after she was given a ticket for the Dance of the Masks, Rue's life became a wild dance of new friends and new scenes. At its centre was John Grey. Both had been masked when they first met. When she had taken off her mask, Rue had decided to hide nothing from John. But could she be sure that he was being as open with her?

RACHEL HIRD

DANCE OF
THE MASKS

Complete and Unabridged

LINFORD
Leicester

First published in Great Britain in 1991 by
Robert Hale Limited
London

First Linford Edition
published 2000
by arrangement with
Robert Hale Limited
London

British Library CIP Data

Hird, Rachel
Dance of the Masks.—Large print ed.—
Linford romance library
1. Love stories
2. Large type books
I. Title
823.9'14 [F]

ISBN 0–7089–5750–1

Published by
F. A. Thorpe (Publishing)
Anstey, Leicestershire

Set by Words & Graphics Ltd.
Anstey, Leicestershire
Printed and bound in Great Britain by
T. J. International Ltd., Padstow, Cornwall

This book is printed on acid-free paper

1

With a squeal of tyres the scruffy little Mini-van juddered round the sharp bend, jerked, and then settled for the long run downhill into the gathering dusk below. Over the howling of the wind there was an abrupt rattling noise, and raindrops appeared and exploded on the windscreen. Rue Morgan sighed, eased her foot off the accelerator and gently touched the brakes. On top of all her other troubles, she didn't need to crash on this lonely part of the Yorkshire Moors.

Expertly Rue drove down into the valley, bounced over the well-known humped bridge and dropped into a lower gear to speed up the other side. The early Spring rain was now torrential, and washed away the dust and mud on the side of the van to show, clearly, the hand-lettered legend

'Rue Morgan — fine eggs, flowers and vegetables'. I'll have to change it, Rue thought bitterly to herself. In future it will be Rue Morgan — unemployed.

For four hours, from past one o'clock until nearly dusk, she had paced alone across the high moors, long legs stretching easily to cover the miles, hoping to find peace in physical exertion. It hadn't come. The sights that normally delighted her had passed unnoticed. All that she could think of was the solicitor's courteous face, apparently quite concerned as he gave her the devastating news. 'I'm sorry Miss Morgan, but you'll have to move out.' Out, Rue thought dully. Out of home, job and future.

Four years ago Bagot's End hadn't seemed a particularly attractive place to live. It was a triangular piece of land, flanked on one side by a muddy road and on the other by a drainage dyke. There was a semi-derelict bungalow made of wood, and half a dozen entirely derelict brick buildings, apparently put up once by the army. It was too small to farm, and just an inconvenient distance from the nearest small town, at the foot of the Yorkshire Moors.

In four years Rue had worked miracles. Buying in help when she couldn't do things herself, she had turned the uninviting site into a neat and efficient market garden, specialising in free range eggs, cut flowers and fresh vegetables. The old brick buildings had been repaired and painted, there were long plastic greenhouses, even the bungalow looked inviting with flowers round it.

Because the site had been unoccupied for over a year when Rue had first leased it she had expected in the fullness of time to buy it. But work came first, money had never worried her overmuch. Perhaps it should have.

Mr Grant, the solicitor, had been scrupulously fair. At his request Rue had driven over to see him, thinking that he intended perhaps to ask her for an increase in rent — something in line with the increase in the cost of living. She would have paid it happily. What he had to say had come as unexpectedly as a thunderbolt.

'I'm afraid your lease has expired. Under the terms we drew up, my clients are entitled to repossess the property now. And this they intend to do.'

Rue had sat in the great leather chair facing him, incapable of speech. 'But you can't do that. It's my home — my living.'

Mr Grant looked uncomfortable. 'You may consult another solicitor of course. Perhaps I should suggest that you do so. But I do feel that he will agree with me. My clients are entitled to possession.'

'I suppose, now it's a going concern, they want to take the business over,' Rue said, anger now replacing shock.

Mr Grant shook his head, and pointed delicately at the local paper on his desk, opened to the property

4

pages. 'Over the past four years house prices around here have rocketed. My clients have obtained outline planning permission for the site. It will be sold for building.'

'So my gardens, my greenhouses, my outbuildings . . .'

'All will be knocked down.'

Somehow, the thought of all her work being torn thoughtlessly to the ground, made her loss even worse. 'Who are these clients?'

He shook his head. 'They wish to remain anonymous.'

'I'm not surprised! Mr Grant, is there nothing I can do? I'll pay double my present rent — even treble.' Rue resented, but couldn't help, the slight tremor in her voice.

'I'll certainly forward your offer. I'll even suggest that perhaps you have been badly treated — though there has been nothing, of course, improper about your lease. Perhaps if you had offered to buy originally . . .'

'I didn't have the money then.

5

Incidentally, what kind of price will it fetch now?'

'It will probably go for auction. But I should think . . . ' He mentioned a figure so ludicrous that Rue had to laugh.

'I doubt I'll be bidding. Thanks for your help Mr Grant. I'll be in touch.' Rue had stumbled down the stairs and into the open street, aware that she had to get away from people for a while, to get somewhere where money wasn't the only reason for living. But this time the moors hadn't helped.

The rain had now steadied to a monotonous downpour, there was a constant rumble on the van roof and the water running across the road swished under her wheels. Suddenly Rue felt tired. I'll be glad to get home, she thought, even if it won't be home for much longer.

For some time now she had been driving with headlights. The darkness was complete, not even the distant lights from a lonely farmhouse pierced the gloom. There was no traffic on the road. Rue felt isolated in her own little universe, knowing there was nobody for miles.

Suddenly there was a flash in her mirror, and after a moment the back of the van was illuminated by the lights of a car, obviously overhauling her rapidly. Rue frowned. She knew this road well, and she thought she was a good driver. Anyone driving at the speed of the lunatic behind was looking for trouble.

The lights were now almost blinding. Obviously, the car was a powerful one. Rue slowed a little and pulled further into the side of the road. With a muted roar the car passed her and swept onwards. Rue thought the dark squat shape was of a Mercedes Sports coupé, but she couldn't be sure. She watched the red tail lights and the white beams slashed by the silver rain. He's going too fast, she thought, he'll never get round the next bend. Unconsciously, she accelerated a little herself.

The tail lights ahead suddenly glared a brighter red as the driver saw how the road bent, and tried in vain to brake. The great headlights seemed for a moment to point straight at the sky, and waved, like a child flashing a torch. Then, they disappeared. He's crashed, Rue thought. The rain drummed down even more fiercely.

Cautiously Rue drew up on the fiercely curving road. Some thirty yards ahead of her, surrounded by heather, was the forlorn looking car, its lights still shining. The driver had been lucky, there was a more or less flat field on the outside of the bend and the car's weight and its sturdy springs had stopped it rolling over. However, there was no sign of life.

'Hello,' Rue called, out of the window, 'are you okay?' There was no answer, and she knew she'd have to go and check.

From the back of the van she pulled her heavy anorak and wriggled into it before getting out. The temperature was several degrees lower than before, and the wind whipped icily round her face. Rue thought several uncharitable thoughts about bad drivers in fast cars. Then she leaned in for her torch and trudged along the swathe in the heather cut by the skidding car.

As she neared it she heard an odd sound, contrasting with the hiss of the rain and the patter of drops on her anorak hood. At first she didn't recognise it, and then the melody asserted itself above the thud of the beat. The car's radio was on — and very loudly indeed. For some reason this made Rue more angry than ever. When she needed music in her Mini-van, she sang.

She bent to peer in the car. There appeared to be just the driver, slumped back in his seat. Rue rapped loudly on the window, and when there was no response, tried the door. It opened.

The music blasted so loudly from the car that Rue jerked back a moment. The second impression was of scent — expensive scent, but rather a lot of it. There could also have been a touch of gin. As the door opened the interior light came on and Rue saw the driver — a girl, perhaps her own age, in an expensive fur lined coat. Her safety belt was still on.

'Are you all right?' Rue queried.

The girl turned and looked at her. 'You do look funny,' she giggled, 'like a wet pixie off the moors.' There was a pause and then she began to sing in time to the music from the radio. 'I've met a pixie, I've met a pixie, I've met a pixie on the moors . . . '

Rue leaned in and switched off the radio. Then she turned and slapped the girl hard on the cheek. For a moment there was no sound but the rain on the roof, then silently the girl began to cry. 'I'm sorry,' she wept, 'but everything's gone wrong. What shall I do?'

Rue trudged round to the passenger side and let herself into the car. The seat was incredibly comfortable, compared with the one in her van.

'We'll just sit here a minute or two and have a little talk,' she said, putting a reassuring arm round the girl's shoulders, 'then we'll set about rescuing you.' The girl laid her head on Rue's wet anorak and wept even harder.

* * *

After a while the sobs and sniffs declined, and the girl sat upright again. She pushed at her hair, reached on to the dashboard for a paper tissue and blew her nose.

'Sorry I slapped you,' Rue said, 'but you did seem a bit hysterical. Now you're more yourself — are you injured at all? Any bruises, anything like that?'

The girl shook her head. 'I did one thing right,' she muttered. 'I put my seat belt on. I'm a bit shaken but otherwise I'm all right.'

'This is the only bend on the road you can run off without crashing. You were lucky.'

'I don't feel very lucky. But I suppose it's good to be alive.' There was a bitterness in the words that made Rue realise that the girl had bigger problems than a car run off the road.

'I'm Rue Morgan,' she said, holding out a hand, 'I'm a market gardener.'

'My name's Fiona Blythe-Whitley,' the girl said shyly, grasping Rue's hand. 'I don't do anything very much. And thank you very much for stopping.'

Rue had switched on the interior light as she sat down. Now she looked at Fiona more carefully. She was dressed to match the car — expensively. Her fur-lined coat hadn't come from a chain store. Under it was a dark blue dress with embroidery round the neck that had to be hand done. The handbag at her side was leather, and had a discreet silver designer symbol. The face however showed no such signs of sophistication. Large earnest blue eyes looked at Rue hopefully, and the quivering mouth might be either petulant or obstinate.

'I don't think we're going to get your car out of here tonight,' Rue said. 'The back wheels are axle deep in mud. It'll need a tractor or something to pull it out.'

Fiona shrugged daintily. 'I'll phone Daddy's firm. They'll send someone out to pick it up. After all, it's the firm's car really.'

'They don't mind you driving it?' Rue asked, incredulously.

'Well, Daddy owns the firm. I get the car as a sort of tax fiddle. 'Cos I'm a director or something, I get paid as well.'

Even though she did a lot of the maintenance herself, the upkeep on Rue's tired old van was one of her chief expenses. 'Wish I had a father like you,' she grumbled. Then she felt angry at herself for being disloyal.

'You wouldn't if you had him,' Fiona retorted with unusual venom. 'He's a pig!'

Rue had been brought up by her father and still mourned his unexpected death five years before. 'Try being without him for a while,' she advised drily, 'and then see if you feel the same way.'

'I'm sorry,' Fiona said humbly, 'but he's responsible for this mess I'm in and I . . .'

Rue recognised the signs of incipient tears. 'Come on,' she said briskly, 'let's get you into my van and I'll drive you to the next village. Is there anything in the back you need to bring?'

'There's all my luggage!' For some reason this made Fiona more upset than ever. Rue sighed and reached for the car keys.

Telling Fiona to stay in the car for the moment, Rue slithered round to the boot and opened it. There she found a set of expensive leather cases and to each of them was tied an airline tag. She bent over and peered at the destination. Fiona was on her way to Los Angeles. Rue shook her head, grabbed the two biggest cases and staggered towards her van. The rain hadn't got any lighter and Rue's mood was not improved when she slipped in the mud and fell full length. She opened the van's back doors and heaved in the cases.

When she got back to the Mercedes Fiona was reaching in the boot, her coat pulled ineffectually over her head. 'I can't let you do everything,' she shouted against the wind, 'it's my fault I'm here.'

'Go and get in the van,' Rue shouted back, 'I'm dressed for this sort of thing, you aren't.' Fiona hesitated for a moment, then when Rue insisted, she gingerly picked her way across the mud. Rue's mood was not improved when she saw that, in spite of tight skirt and high heels, Fiona did not fall flat as she had.

It took Rue another two journeys to fetch all she intended out of the Mercedes. Finally she switched off the lights, wound up the windows and locked the car. Now it was all up to Fiona's Daddy's firm. Feeling aggrieved and wet Rue sloshed back to the van.

In the half hour or so since Rue had stopped, nothing else had come along the road. Rue hadn't expected it to, she had picked the route because it was lonely. Fastening herself in her seat belt, Rue started the van and set off cautiously down the hill. The heater did its best to dispel the fug that soon grew inside, but like much of the rest of the van it was past its best.

'Where were you going Fiona?' she asked after a while, suspecting that the miserable figure next to her would not speak unless spoken to first. 'Woodley's about twelve miles away. You can arrange about your car there. Is there anyone who can pick you up — d'you want to phone home?'

Fiona peered at her tiny jewelled watch. 'I was going to Tees-side Airport,' she said sadly. 'I've got a ticket down to Stanstead on the seven o'clock plane, and I was going to catch a connection for Los Angeles tonight.

My . . . my boyfriend will be waiting for me at Stanstead. If I'm not there, he'll go without me.'

'Phone him,' Rue snorted. 'Explain to him that you've had an accident. He'll wait for you.'

Fiona shook her head. 'He won't. I've let him down so many times that he won't believe me. He thinks I'm under Daddy's thumb — and I am. We wanted to get engaged but Daddy said we had to wait two years — till Peter comes back from America. He's got a job as an architect there. But this time I thought I'd just managed it. Daddy flew to Geneva this morning, and what he said to me first made me really mad. So I phoned Peter, and he said if I was there at midnight we'd go together. He'd get me a ticket. But I won't be there and he'll go without me.'

'Fly on after him,' Rue exploded.

'You don't know me like I do. I'm a pushover for family pressure. I dithered packing — that's why I was taking a

17

short-cut and driving so fast in the car. But I thought I could get there in time.'

Rue sighed. She was wet, tired and had problems of her own. Fiona was, quite frankly, a wimp. And anyone who treated money with the carelessness that she did didn't deserve much sympathy. But still . . . Rue hastily thought of the roads between here and Stockton. If she could get over on to the A19 in time.

'I'll try and get you to the airport by seven o'clock. It'll be a strain — but it's possible.'

'You will! That's fantastic! Oh Rue, if you could I'd . . . of course I'll pay . . .'

'Don't say it,' Rue interrupted curtly, 'or you'll be out at Woodley. I'm a market gardener, not a taxi driver.'

'I'm sorry,' Fiona apologised humbly. 'I come from a family that thinks money will solve anything.'

'It has its uses.'

While they crossed the moors Rue had to concentrate on her driving,

Fiona realised this and said little. But in time they dropped out of the hills and on to wider, better-lit roads and she relaxed a little. By her side Fiona was obviously happier. When Rue glanced at her she was smiling, and from time to time she hummed to herself. Rue felt a reluctant pleasure at having made someone happy.

'So what did your father do to give you the strength to defy him like this?'

'I never thought I could. He's got lots of money, and he's always flying all over the place, apparently to get more. Well, he invited this man from London to come up and stay the weekend. He was really chuffed, cos this man doesn't visit very much, and Daddy had to impress him. He was meeting him at this big charity do on Saturday night. It's a masked ball, all the county's coming. Then Daddy found he just couldn't make it, he had to go to Geneva. So he told me I'd have to go. And he told me I had to be nice to the man. When I told him I was practically an engaged girl he shouted at me and said I'd done nothing all my life, I could do something useful for once. So I waited till he'd gone and phoned Peter.'

'Good for you,' Rue said briefly, rather sympathetic to this odd girl. 'I hope everything works out for you.'

'It will, 'cos of you. You've made it all work out.' Rue smiled, ironically wondering if she could work out her own problems.

Two minutes later they drove on to the A19. 'We're going to make it, I think,' Rue commented. 'Just be sure this is what you want to do.'

'Oh it is!' After that there was silence.

* * *

Once they had entered the airport Rue saw Fiona change into a different creature, obviously accustomed to flying around the world, and assured of the power her credit cards and cash could give her. Not even the muddy shoes and wet coat dented her confidence. She was in time for her plane, her baggage was efficiently dispatched. In the bright lights Rue looked at her more closely. Fiona was taller than she had thought — almost as tall — five feet ten inches — as Rue herself.

'We're both big girls,' she smiled at Fiona.

'We are. I stoop a lot though. Daddy sent me to all sorts of places to try and get me to act tall. I wish I could walk with your confidence.'

'How tall is Peter?'

'Six foot two. I couldn't go out with a man smaller than myself.' Rue sympathised.

'Rue, I've got an idea! I want to give you something.'

'I've told you, I've done this for love.'

'Not money, I've got a better idea. Look here.' Fiona thrust two boxes towards Rue. Rue recognised the black and silver packing as coming from the very best ladies' outfitters in York. She couldn't even afford a handkerchief from there.

'This is a dress — a new one — for the masked ball on Saturday. And it would fit you. In this little box is a mask. Why don't you take them and go in my place?'

Rue laughed, and gently pushed the two boxes away. 'Don't be silly, I couldn't. Besides, this dress must have cost a fortune.'

'Daddy ordered it specially for the ball. Nothing he could do would make me wear it — ever.'

'But . . . but people would know I wasn't you. This man that's coming.'

'He's never met me. And I hardly know anyone there. I told you Daddy couldn't come. Besides, everyone's got to be masked. If you've got an invitation you get in.'

'An invitation . . .'

'I've got it here.' Fiona scrabbled in her handbag, produced a large red envelope and gave it to Rue. 'Please take it. You don't know how much you've helped me.' Behind them, the loudspeakers announced Fiona's flight.

'I don't know . . . '

'Rue Morgan you're wonderful. I'll look you up when I come back from America. Now go to the ball. Bye . . . ' Waving, Fiona turned and was gone.

Picking up the two boxes, and pocketing the invitation, Rue sighed, and walked back towards her van. As she drove out of the airport, a plane roared overhead. Rue wished she could run away from her problems like that. It was time to go home.

★ ★ ★

For some reason the fifty mile drive back to Bagot's End seemed depressing. The van had seemed out of place among the shining cars in the airport, and Rue was conscious of being cold, wet and hungry. She would be glad to get home. The rain diminished slightly, instead of the quite exhilarating downpour there was only a miserable drizzle. For the moment, Rue forgot about Fiona and thought of her own problems.

Eventually she reached home. It had never seemed so inviting, even in the rain, as now she knew she'd have to lose it.

Behind the front door was a note, evidently pushed through the letter box. 'Waited an hour. Have gone to Red Lion. Hope to see you there. Barry.' Rue sighed. She'd only said she might go out for a drink tonight, and Barry was to phone her first. She guessed he'd arrived without ringing first, knowing it was harder to resist an invitation when someone was on your doorstep, than when they were on the end of a telephone. And this time he'd been unlucky. Well tough. He'd been told to ring.

Rue stripped off her damp clothing and ran a bath. While it was filling she made herself a mug of coffee and a cheese sandwich. Although she didn't particularly want to go out, she guessed she owed it to Barry. And there weren't all that many men these days that invited her out. Like Fiona, she didn't want to tower over her escort, and her work kept her from meeting the kind of man that would interest her. Barry had been vaguely on the scene for a while now, but vaguely was the important word.

Half an hour later she drove to the Red Lion. It was a pub on the outskirts of town, much patronised by the younger, well-to-do crowd, who all seemed to have gone to the local school together. Rue knew many of them, but she wasn't impressed by most.

'There's my girl! Over here, tall red-haired and beautiful!'

Rue sighed. Barry was with his boisterous friends, and had obviously had a little too much to drink already.

'I'll get you a drink. You've got a lot of catching up to do. Find yourself a seat.'

'I'd like a . . . ' But Barry had already gone. Rue perched on the edge of a bench and listened to the noisy conversation, concentrated as it usually was on local gossip and the price of everything. Barry was a surveyor, and they seemed to spend most of their time together cultivating the solicitors, farmers and builders who put work his way. Rue watched him concentrate as he carried a tray from the bar to their table. She was certain now he'd had too much. He was tall and broad, with just the suggestion of a paunch bulging over his belt. Sadly, Rue realised that in another ten years he'd be fat. Even more sadly, she realised that she didn't really care, she wouldn't be around to see it.

'This is for you darling.' He placed a tall glass in front of her and fumbled a kiss on her cheek. Rue sipped; it was gin and tonic.

'How much gin is there in here?'

'Only just enough. Like I said, you've got a lot of catching up to do.' There

26

was a roar of laughter behind them as someone spilled a pint of beer over the table. Rue sipped again. She guessed there was at least a treble in the glass. Barry's idea of seduction tended to be of the grossest kind.

When they drove away an hour later Rue left two full glasses on the table. Barry had complained bitterly; someone else had grabbed them and swallowed them, but Rue didn't care. They'd left Barry's car in the park and she was driving him home.

'I had a bit of bad news today,' she said, changing gear and removing Barry's hand from her thigh. 'It looks like I'll have to give up the smallholding.'

Barry didn't care for her working so hard and so often, but he ought to have known what the place meant to her. Apparently he didn't.

'Good,' he said promptly. 'Now you'll have to come and work for me as a receptionist.'

Rue winced. 'I don't want to be a

27

receptionist and I don't want to work for you. I love plants.'

Barry laughed. 'It looks like you'll have to give it up. Anyway, I don't like my girlfriend spending all her time up to her armpits in earth and dirt. What d'you think my friends will think?'

'I'm not sure that I really care what your friends think,' Rue said in a quiet voice that should have warned him. It didn't.

'We'll get you a job somehow. I'll have a word with old Ronnie Scott at the Town Hall. He owes me a favour, he'll fit you in somewhere. He's always looking out for new staff.'

'How kind of him.'

They were drawing up outside the large semi that Barry shared with his mother. 'Oh blast,' Barry said. 'The old trout's still up. It means we can't go in. Drive round the corner where it's darker, Rue.'

'What for?' Rue queried, pulling directly under a street light.

'Well, if you don't mind being seen

28

I suppose I don't.' Barry lunged across the cab and pressed his beery mouth on to hers. At the same time his hand ran up her thigh.

'Get off Barry!' Usually Barry did as he was told, but this time he didn't.

The crack of Rue's hand against his face echoed through the little van. Rue wondered gloomily if it had been heard in the street outside.

'What did you do that for! It hurt!'

'It was meant to. Now get out before I lose my temper.'

'If I get out now, I never get in this van again,' Barry blustered.

Rue leaned over him and opened the passenger door. 'You said it Barry. Goodbye. We'll not meet again.'

'But . . . '

'Get out!'

Barry stumbled out of the van, and watched amazed as it accelerated down the street. 'Bloody woman,' he cursed and fumbled for his keys.

It took Rue ten minutes to drive home. She made herself cocoa and another cheese sandwich then put her feet up on the settee and flicked on her cassette player. There was a hiss and one of her favourite tapes came on — Frank Sinatra singing *Songs for Swinging Lovers*. Rue grinned. What a day, she thought.

2

Rue's day started early every morning so the next one should not have been a strain. However, she was worried over where she would live and where she would work. As she set off down the path in the early morning darkness, bundled up against the cold and clutching her second mug of tea, there didn't seem to be much point to what she was doing. Why should she get up two hours before normal human beings, for a very moderate payment, and see all her hard work being ruined at the whim of some builder?

And there was Barry. She didn't intend to see him again. To be honest, Rue thought to herself, he wasn't much of a loss, but hers was a solitary life and she needed some friends. She picked up her plastic bucket and opened the gate in the wire netting fence. Roosting hens peered at her furtively and cooed as she entered the old building she'd converted into a henhouse. As always the search for eggs, still warm from the straw, cheered Rue up. Stop feeling sorry for yourself, she thought. It's a miserable emotion.

When the bucket was nearly full with eggs Rue went into the first greenhouse. She moved efficiently down the aisle, cutting the early salads, and then picking vegetables from the other greenhouses. Everything was placed neatly in plastic trays. She checked a small handwritten list and selected sheaves of spring flowers. Lastly she visited the herb garden and snipped what seemed freshest. An hour after she had started, Rue had loaded her van and was driving towards the main road.

Not many people passed Bagot's End, so there was no point in Rue trying to run a farm shop. Besides, she was interested in growing, not selling. She thought herself lucky in that three of the large hotels in the area would take all the fresh vegetables she could deliver, and a fair amount of the flowers. Payment was regular, if not too generous, and there was no hassle.

Rue parked well away from the first hotel and carried two trays round to the kitchen entrance. The rich guests of Dale View Hotel were not to be disturbed by buzzing delivery vans in the early hours. Parker's Hotel came next, and then by nine o'clock she was at the Sir Charles Dover Hotel, her third and last call, and gratefully accepted a cup of coffee in the kitchen.

'This is good, is good,' Luigi, the Italian chef said, eagerly rummaging through the trays Rue had brought. 'Tonight I shall offer just a simple salad — with my finest olive oil.' He cracked a baby carrot in half and tasted it. 'With these ingredients — cooking is a pleasure — in fact cooking is not necessary.'

Rue smiled at him. 'Don't let the

manager hear you say that. He might think he can do without you.'

Luigi sniffed. 'Our important Mr Dermot thinks that hotels are run from the cash desk. He should learn that people come here to eat our food, not to pay his bills. And did you ask him for more money as I told you?'

'I asked,' Rue confessed. 'He said that he was on a very tight budget and that fresh ingredients like mine were really a luxury.'

'He better not say that to me!' Luigi snarled.

'Don't worry and don't say anything,' Rue told him. 'I'll supply you as long as I can.' She swallowed her coffee and stood. 'Work calls.'

'Here are your empty trays,' Luigi said, thrusting a parcel between two of them. 'I've put in a few scraps here — for the hens, you understand.'

'Luigi!' Rue said warningly. 'I ate like a queen on the last parcel you gave me.'

'I am the chef here,' Luigi said

34

haughtily. 'If I say they're scraps — then they are!' He winked. Rue sighed, smiled and left.

★ ★ ★

After working hard all morning Rue always had a long lunch break. Today she opened Luigi's parcel and found fresh bread — baked that very morning. With some Italian sausage he'd also included, she made herself a salad. Feeling comfortably full afterwards she wandered into her bedroom in search of a book. By the side of the bed were the two packages given to her yesterday by Fiona. Rue frowned. So much seemed to have happened that she'd almost forgotten yesterday's trip to the airport. She picked up the larger package and stripped off the expensive black and silver wrapping.

Under the outer cover was a cardboard box, and in it layers of tissue. Feeling like a child opening Christmas presents, Rue tore at the white stuff.

Under it all was a full length evening gown. Almost reverently Rue picked it up by the straps and was about to hold it against her. Then she winced, placed the dress carefully on the bed and ran to her bathroom. Five minutes later she was showered and dried, her hair pinned up and wearing fresh underwear. Then she took up the dress again.

It was a kingfisher blue in colour, that altered in shade as Rue handled it. It felt fine and soft, and looked like suede; Rue guessed it was raw silk. She lifted it over her head and slipped into it. She shook the skirt, getting the dress to hang right, then turned to look at herself in the full length mirror on the old wardrobe.

The bra would have to go. It showed over and to the side of the dress — which was largely backless. Rue wriggled and twisted to take it off, then readjusted the top and looked at herself again. It fitted perfectly. A faint blush touched her sun-browned face and body. Rue wasn't vain but she knew she looked gorgeous.

Since she'd left college Rue had had little chance of dressing up. All her work was messy, so she tended to wear slacks and a T-shirt that progressively got filthier as the day wore on. At night she wore neat simple outfits that looked all right, but weren't very exciting. This dress looked expensive, frivolous; suggested a lifestyle that was entirely foreign to Rue. As she looked at herself in the mirror one thing was certain. She was going to wear that dress.

The smaller box held the mask. Rue opened it, shook off the wrappers and looked. It was a confection of light blue silk spotted with black. Rue recognised the French clown, Pierrette. She pulled it on. The mask came down to mid face, covering much of her hair, her eyes and nose, but leaving her mouth uncovered. A mysterious, gay creature stared at Rue from the speckled mirror, clad in a shimmering blue dress with a haunting half mask above it. Rue smiled, through sheer joy. Her reflected image smiled back, enigmatically. I must buy new shoes, she thought.

The name on the engraved invitation was simple — Pierrette. The dance was to be held by courtesy of Lord de Fearn at Wenton Hall. No one would be allowed in unless masked — and there would be a grand unmasking at midnight. Rue tapped the invitation and reached for her road atlas. She had a feeling that Wenton Hall was about fifteen miles away. She could get there easily.

Once her mind was made up Rue pressed on with her preparations. At College she'd been ever ready for any scatter-brained plan that her friends could come up with. It struck her that she'd got a bit stodgy in the past five years. Life had been all work and nothing else. She needed a touch of excitement, a touch of danger almost. So if she was going to the ball, she was going in style.

Three days later Rue drove sedately

through country lanes towards Wenton Hall. She had borrowed her uncle's Austin Maestro; it struck her that to arrive in her scruffy van might look a little strange at such an obviously expensive ball. As she maintained her dignified thirty-five miles an hour she noticed that she was in a little convoy. The car in front was a dark green Rolls-Royce, and the one behind appeared to be a black Daimler. Hmmm thought Rue.

She'd finished all her work by midday that day and spent a blissful afternoon pampering herself. First had been one of her rare visits to the hairdresser who had fallen in love with the mask, and worked out a style in which Rue's rich brown hair cascaded down her back, instead of being screwed up tightly in a bun. Then there'd been an hour soaking and luxuriating in the bath, with a frantic scrubbing at her fingers to get out the dirt that somehow always seemed to penetrate her gardening gloves. She'd bought new briefs, new tights, a tiny bottle of perfume, a handbag and a pair of high-heeled dancing shoes, the price of which still made her wince. And she'd sat for half an hour in front of her mirror, listening to her favourite Frank Sinatra tapes and carefully putting on her make-up. In fact with the mask on there had been little to do; just lipstick and a touch of mascara. She had thought about jewellery and finally decided to wear none at all. The dress and the mask were sufficient. Besides, what did she have? Then a quick look through the curtains and a cautious dash across the lawn into the car. The pensioner couple down the road, Harry and Madge Allen, were old friends. But for some reason Rue didn't want anyone to see her like this.

* * *

The Rolls in front slowed down and Rue realised they were approaching large gates and a small grey gatehouse.

When the Rolls stopped she fumbled on the seat beside her and pulled on her mask. The Rolls drove on and she was flagged down by one of two men wearing dark green uniforms with the name of a security firm on the shoulder.

'Good evening Ma'am. If I could just see your invitation please?'

Rue felt confident and concealed behind her mask, and handed over the black envelope. 'You're being very conscientious tonight.'

The man flipped over a page on a checkboard and ticked something off. 'Orders Ma'am. We've had to turn away two gatecrashers already. Dressed, in masks, everything. Claimed they'd forgotten their tickets — but wouldn't give their names.' He smiled briefly. 'We've got everything double checked here. Now, if you drive straight forward to the front of the house, one of our men will help you park. I hope you enjoy your evening.' He gave her a half salute and Rue drove on, excitement and apprehension churning in her stomach. She hadn't done anything like this for years!

Wenton Hall was at the end of a long curving drive. Although the gatehouse had obviously been very well kept, Rue's gardener's eye saw that the grounds could do with quite a lot of attention. She supposed few people now could afford the number of workers needed to keep such a place perfect. The house itself was grey and elegant, with the beautifully proportioned windows that meant it was Georgian. To one side Rue could see a brightly coloured marquee. As she stopped on the gravel forecourt another courteous security guard stepped forward and offered to park the car. Rue smiled and he made no objection when she said she'd rather do it herself. The Maestro was a nice car, but it looked a little out of place when lined up with the glistening monsters already in the park. Rue shivered a little, checked her appearance in the mirror and got out. Now for it. She walked round to the front doors.

Two large cars had just pulled up and Rue walked casually towards the crowd that was chatting on the front steps and then followed them in. Everyone was masked, in a variety of ornate styles. One or two wore simple highwayman masks in black velvet. But one lady had a superb peacock mask, with the colours of the feathers picked out in her dress. All the men were in dinner jackets and the women — Rue realised her dress was not out of place. She was also glad she'd decided not to wear any of her few pieces of costume jewellery; she saw rings, a diamond tiara, a pearl necklace, all with that indefinable presence which said they were real. No wonder there were so many security guards.

They entered the hall. Rue had a quick glimpse of panelled walls, of paintings, obviously of somebody's ancestors, of a central table with a beautiful arrangement of flowers.

Then she followed her little group into an ante-room which had been turned into a ladies' cloakroom. Rue took one glance at herself in a mirror and decided she'd do. Idly she listened to the chatter around her.

' . . . so with this scare about sunburn being bad for one, we decided that the Caribbean was completely out,' a middle aged lady was declaring. 'I just don't know where we'll go this summer. It's an insoluble problem.'

Try Scarborough, Rue thought, but said nothing. Judging by the emeralds around the woman's neck, she might possibly own the town.

'We're going cruising with Henry in the Med,' another lady offered. 'He's still got that awful boat of his — no one will buy it, so he has to get some use out of it.'

A communal mutter seemed to agree that this was the best solution.

The first woman finished applying her lipstick and stood. She turned and smiled at Rue, obviously intending to make sure the single girl wasn't left out of the conversation. 'Holidays are a problem aren't they my dear?' she asked courteously.

'I spend an awful long time thinking where I'd like to go,' Rue confessed, and then fled before she had to admit she hadn't actually been anywhere for the last five years. This was a new world.

More people were entering the hall now, and Rue found no problem in following them as they walked through double doors into what was obviously the dining room. A buffet had been laid out at one end of the room, and as Rue entered, a waiter presented her with a slender flute of champagne. She sipped. It was rather nice. From the far end of the room there were sounds of a dance band, and Rue saw that further double doors opened into the marquee. She put down her empty glass and drifted towards them.

No expense had been spared in the marquee. Great swags of pink and white cloth lined the canvas of the walls and roof, a wooden floor had been laid and a band played discreetly on a dais at one end. Small tables, each with a pure white cloth and a vase of flowers, dotted the outer edge.

Rue sat, a little self consciously, at a table just inside the marquee. She had not really thought through the problems of coming, masked, to a dance with neither partner nor friend. Most of the guests appeared to be in couples or in parties, though there were a few men striding about, apparently unattached. Anyway, the problem of dancing or talking with a man was likely to be as big as the problem of having no partner at all. For a moment Rue worried, and then she grinned. Any problem she could deal with. She'd already caught a few admiring glances from passing men, and knew that although the dress was eye-catching, so was she.

A few couples were on the floor now, and Rue noticed one in particular. A tall heavily-built man was dancing with a slim woman in a silver and white dress and a mask made of some fine flowing material. As they came closer, twirling expertly, Rue saw that the mask was of a butterfly. The pair danced gracefully together, the woman especially obviously enjoying herself. They came closer still, and Rue saw with something of a shock that she was quite old. Although from a distance she had the figure and the movements of a young woman, yet her skin had the fineness and translucence that only age could bring.

A long chord from the band signalled the end of the dance. With a final pirouette the woman sank in a curtsy and the man bowed to her. Then he took her arm and they walked together to a table to greet friends. Rue wondered idly what she herself would be like when she got old. She hoped she'd have the same joy in life as this old lady.

The band struck up again, and with a slight feeling of panic Rue saw that the well-built man was walking towards her. He stopped, bent his head and said in a cheerful voice, 'One of the privileges of lending your house for a charity ball is that you get to dance with all the pretty young ladies. Might I have this dance please?'

Rue liked his mixture of happiness and formality. She rose and stepped towards him. 'I'd love to dance. But I don't think I will do half as well as your last partner.'

Like one or two of the other men, her partner had opted to wear a very simple mask, a single strip of black velvet round his eyes. When he smiled at Rue's compliment she could see that it brought him obvious pleasure. 'Mother loves dancing. When you young things are giving up she'll still be on the floor, demanding another five minutes.'

'I was just hoping I'd be as fit when I was her age.'

Expertly the man whirled her down the floor. 'Just keep dancing. It must do you good.'

Rue laughed, then abandoned herself to the rhythm.

She loved both physical exercise and most music, and this combination of the two always exhilarated her. Her partner sensed her enjoyment and didn't speak again, concentrating solely on guiding her. It was with a feeling of regret that Rue heard the last chord of the dance.

Courteously her partner walked her back to the empty table. 'On your own?' he asked with a smile, 'Surely you must have an escort somewhere? Would you care to come and join us?'

It was the last thing Rue wanted, although she responded to the thoughtfulness of the man. She blushed a little as she lied, 'My partner will be here shortly. Business called him. Even on an evening like this.'

'Then I'll leave you. I'm sure you'll not be alone for long.' With another half bow the man walked away. He was older than Rue — in his mid forties, she thought, and she'd really liked him.

Quickly she slipped back into the dining room, not wanting to stay so obviously on her own. She accepted another glass of champagne and wrinkled her nose as the bubbles made her want to sneeze. I could get to like being rich, she thought, it has definite advantages.

More people were now walking through the room, and Rue decided to wait until the marquee filled up a little. To avoid being noticed she took her glass and looked at one of the pictures on the wall, a late Victorian study of flowers. She was appreciating the delicacy of the water colours when . . .

'Good evening Pierrette.' A male voice behind her, low and musical, but even in those three words Rue thought she could detect a hint of irony.

She turned. Her first, almost pointless thought, was one of pleasure. The man was taller than her. Like all the other men there he was clad in the black and white of evening dress but with one touch of colour, a blood red rose in his lapel. Lean hips and waist swept upwards to broad shoulders. Rue shivered as she looked at the mask. It was almost the same as hers — but with lines that made it obviously masculine. This was Pierrot to her Pierrette.

'I'm sorry I couldn't pick you up at home but you know what business is like,' the man continued. 'I've just driven up from London.'

'You must be tired,' Rue faltered.

The man shrugged. 'Your father was most apologetic about not being here — but also most insistent that I come anyway. He sent me this mask — and said you'd look after me.'

Rue eyed the man silently a moment. She remembered what Fiona had said — that her father insisted she go to the dance to be nice to this man. Well, with any luck Fiona was now with her Peter in America. And Rue had no intention of being nice to anyone she didn't like. Besides, everything this man had said so far had been ironic. He didn't like having arrangements made for him.

'I'll certainly look after you,' she said briskly. 'Why don't you sit down and I'll fetch you a plate of something and see if I can get a cup of tea.'

Under the half mask Rue could see a clean cut chin and a mouth, generous and curved, but so far unsmiling. Now it twitched. 'Thank you. But when I'm ready I think I'll have the strength to get to the table myself.'

There was another pause and the two eyed each other, each wondering what thoughts the other's mask concealed. 'Fiona, isn't it?' The man broke the silence.

Rue lifted her hand to her mask. 'This is a masked ball. Until midnight I'm Pierrette. Until midnight names, positions, money don't count. I've come here to dance.'

'Not a point of view your father would agree with. He thinks like me. Names and position can be bought — but money always counts.'

There was an air of cynicism in the way he said it; Rue guessed that he knew why Fiona's father was so anxious he should partner her. She turned and pointed at the picture behind her. 'I was admiring this picture,' she said, 'I think it's quite beautiful. What d'you think its value is?'

The man looked at her and Rue could feel the contempt in the half hidden eyes. 'I don't usually assess my host's goods, but I should imagine about two thousand pounds.'

'I thought you'd say that,' Rue said, mock-mournfully. 'Pierrot I asked you for value and you gave me price. I'm sorry for anyone who can't tell the difference. Good evening Pierrot. Somewhere here I'm sure you'll find a partner who shares your interest in cash. But I don't.'

The man hardly moved, but menace flowed from him, in the flexed shoulders and hawk-like poise of the head. Rue stepped forward and . . .

53

'John! You managed to make it! It's good to see you.' To Rue's surprise the heavily-built man she'd danced with earlier came up to them and forcefully grasped the hand of her antagonist.

'You know me Charlie. I love it here.'

'And trust you to bring a beautiful young lady. She dances like an angel.'

Masked eyes looked at Rue speculatively. 'I'm still looking forward to that pleasure.'

'I'll leave you two to talk,' Rue put in hastily, 'I'll just go and comb my hair.' Before either of them could object she moved past them and headed for the ladies' cloakroom. This evening was providing her with more shocks than she could easily cope with.

In the cloakroom she looked at herself in the mirror. The little fight with — John was it? — had made her pulses race. Her eyes were bright and there was a delicate flush on her cheeks. For a moment she wondered if she ought to head straight out of the building and go home. Then she snarled to herself. She was staying.

There was only one figure in the hall outside the cloakroom. John was sitting on a chair by the central table. He rose as he saw Rue. 'There's no way a man can wait outside a ladies' cloakroom with dignity,' he remarked as Rue looked at him hesitantly. 'And because you've put me to that embarrassment, I think the least you can do is dance with me once.'

Rue found herself giggling. 'Do you embarrass easily?' she asked demurely.

'Not usually. But I'll make an exception in your case.'

'Then I'd love to dance — Pierrot.'

'This way — Pierrette.'

There were more in the marquee now but it still wasn't crowded and John swept her easily across the floor. She had thought the other man — Charlie — had been a good dancer, but John was better. As they spun round a corner Rue forgot where she was, and closed her eyes in the sheer ecstasy of movement. She opened them to find her partner studying her intently. 'You like dancing?' It was more a statement than a question.

'I love it,' Rue confessed.

'Then you'll stay with me?'

'Pierrette is Pierrot's partner — at least for the night.'

John appeared to accept Rue's ground rules quite happily. Not once did he mention the reason he thought she was there, nor talk about his work. Instead they chatted about music, about the moors, about what was happening in the news. After an hour they paused and Rue ate heartily from the magnificent buffet.

'I like a girl who doesn't pick at her food,' John said approvingly as Rue helped herself to more salmon.

'There's a lot of me,' Rue grinned.

'I can see a lot of you.' John ran his finger lightly down her naked back and Rue was shocked by the feeling of excitement it gave her. 'You're beautifully brown and there are no bikini marks. You must have been sunbathing topless. The south of France?'

'My garden,' Rue admitted, honestly.

'And here there are four tiny moles. Do you know that poem by John Donne called *Love's Progress*?'

'Yes I know it. And let me tell you Pierrot, you aren't getting embayed anywhere.'

'That is a pity.' The two of them sat silent a moment, each aware that they'd strayed into something quite new.

'John Grey, there's a call for you in the library. It's from your man in London. And when you come out you can dance with me at least once.' Shocked by the sudden intrusion, the two turned to look at the girl who had spoken.

She was shorter than Rue, and dressed in red velvet which didn't do a lot for her rather ample figure. Rue thought her mask — a rather spiteful looking cat — suited her tone of voice admirably.

'I'll come over and say hello to you all later,' John said, with steely politeness.

'You do. And then you can introduce us to your partner. It's not like you to let yourself be monopolised.'

'This is Pierrette, who is lovely. Anyone would let themselves be monopolised by her.'

'I'm sure.' The girl stamped away.

'Marsha likes getting her own way,' John said, winking at Rue. 'Unfortunately, so do I. Come on, I've been half expecting this call. There's no rest for us money-makers.' He led her out of the dining room and into the library.

'Isn't it a bit late for a business call?' Rue had to ask.

'It might be nearly midnight here. What time d'you think it is in Tokyo?'

At first there seemed to be something incongruous in a man dressed in a Pierrot's mask talking on the telephone to someone in London about the price of shares in Tokyo. Rue sat at the table and listened, fascinated. John was asking for information, thinking, then issuing quick curt instructions. Rue realised with a shock that he had almost forgotten she was there, so completely absorbed was he in his decision making. The sight of such intensity and dedication rather frightened her. But eventually he finished and glanced at his thin white-gold watch.

'I think we've time for just one more dance, Pierrette,' he said. 'And then it will be midnight — and time to unmask.'

'I'd like another dance,' Rue said, hoping that the sadness she felt wasn't obvious.

For the last time they swirled round the ballroom. Then there was a roll on the drums and Charlie stepped up on to the small stage.

'Ladies and Gentlemen, it is nearly midnight. Soon you may see who you have been dancing with. When the clock strikes twelve you must all unmask.'

Almost reluctantly John released Rue,

and stepped back a pace. Rue turned and looked behind her. All the lights went out. There was a single loud beat on a drum. 'One,' the crowd shouted. Rue slipped out of her shoes and bent to pick them up. 'Two,' the crowd shouted at the next beat. Rue leaned forward, felt for John and kissed him lightly. 'Three.' Rue turned and walked quickly and silently along her memorised path. 'Four.' She moved quickly through the dining room and into the hall. 'Five.' One of the security guards at the front door looked at her in surprise.

Rue had just got in her car when the light flashed on in the marquee. There was a roar of delight from the crowd inside. Gently, Rue drove forward. Her car was checked again at the gatehouse, but two minutes later she was on the road, leaving Wenton Hall behind her.

3

Rue drove home cautiously through the narrow winding lanes, conscious that she'd had several glasses of champagne and that it wasn't her car. Once back at Bagot's End she stepped carefully out of the blue dress, and hung it, covered with a polythene bag, in her wardrobe. She wondered how she'd get it back to Fiona. Borrowing the dress was one thing, there was no way she could really keep it. As she climbed into her bath, clutching her customary mug of cocoa, she recognised that her rather madcap evening was going to have all sorts of consequences she hadn't quite thought through.

You're just stuck on that John Grey, she muttered to herself, and then realised the blush on her face and shoulders came from more than the heat of the water. So, John Grey had

had an effect on her. What did she think of him?

He was tall dark and handsome. The trite little saying made Rue smile but it was true. Compared with him, Barry came nowhere. For a moment Rue wondered if she was attracted to John on the rebound from Barry, but then decided that Barry had never meant much to her.

After their initial argument, Rue had found John to be witty and excellent company. He was a good dancer. He liked music. Why then was she dubious about him? Apart from the description of him that Fiona had given, Rue realised that it was the time that he had spent on the phone in the library that had unsettled her. His complete concentration on what he was saying had been alien to Rue. She couldn't imagine being so single-minded about anything, and especially about making money. The very idea of a masked man earning a living by giving instructions to a lackey in London about share prices in Tokyo . . . Rue giggled. She knew all about the price of spring flowers and early season fresh vegetables. That was the real world.

She sank further into the bath and paddled her feet so that tiny waves lapped under her chin. Anyway, he didn't even know her name or where she lived. They would never meet again. Rue didn't ask herself why this thought was vaguely unpleasant.

★ ★ ★

At lunchtime on Monday Rue drove the eight miles to the village of Enton to return her uncle's car. He was her only living relative; her father's brother, and, in his undemonstrative way, very fond of her. He opened the door of his stone-built cottage, the bristling moustache, erect body and highly polished shoes suggesting the soldier he'd been for so long.

'We're back,' she said, kissing him, 'I've filled up with petrol and there's not a scratch anywhere.'

'Hmm. I suppose you're not a bad driver — for a woman.'

Rue grinned. Uncle Tom was a bachelor who had spent thirty five years of his life in the army. He still firmly believed that a woman's place was in the home, and a man's place was at work. When Rue suggested to him that things might have altered a little, he placidly said that he was too old to change his mind.

'Your garden's looking well,' she commented, peering through the window at the regimented square in front, 'I've brought you a few plants. There's some bronze fennel that'll grow to six feet. And some saxifrage and some cascading helianthemum. They should make a good splash of colour by summer.'

'At their best about the beginning of July?' The voice was excited.

'I know what you want them for. You'll have the best show in the village by judging day.'

'Superb. Thank you very much my

dear. I'll have them planted by this evening.'

'Perhaps I could dig . . .'

'Certainly not,' her uncle said with finality. 'Other people may accept help. But my garden is my garden. If I win the competition I'll win fairly.'

'You'll win this year.' With her face to the window, Rue suppressed a smile. The village was noted for its gardens. Once a year there was a competition to select the cottage that had the best show, and the rivalry was intense. Old friends like her uncle, the vicar and postmistress grew short with each other until judging day was over. Her uncle had won three times and been second five times. He was ready for another win.

Rue moved to an easy chair in front of the fire and sat facing Tom. 'Did you get anywhere with finding out who's buying my land?'

He sniffed. 'You were a fool not to buy when you moved in. I offered you the money.'

'I know you did and you know that I couldn't have accepted. Now what have you found out?' Ex-Brigadier Tom Morgan had a network of surprisingly highly placed friends throughout the district; there wasn't much he couldn't worm out in time.

'Nothing yet but it's still early days. I was told one thing. That land is worth a small fortune as a building plot. Running it as a nursery, with the turnover you have, is economic nonsense.'

She sighed. 'Is economic sense the only kind there is?'

'No,' the old man said gently, 'but you're in this world and you've got to live in it.' They both sat silent a moment, obviously thinking the same thing. There were lines in Tom's face that reminded Rue of her father, a younger and gentler man who never had the toughness of his older brother.

'Chasing money isn't my idea of living.'

'Perhaps not but . . . what's the matter?'

Her uncle despised lace curtains. From her seat by the fire Rue could see clearly out of the window and across the well-kept village green. A large and expensive car, a maroon Jaguar, had just drawn up outside the post office. From it a man climbed and moved towards the little shop. There was no mistaking that build or that walk. It was John Grey. Wildly Rue wondered if his appearing might just be a coincidence, but she knew better. Somehow he'd traced her.

It had been a normal hard-working day for her, and she was still dressed in the dusty sweater and jeans she used to make her deliveries. Her hair was tied up in a bun and her face was innocent of make-up. The last thing she wanted was to meet John. As she stared, hypnotised, across the green, the man came out of the post office and walked purposefully towards the cottage. He was going to call.

'You look as if you've seen a ghost,' Tom said testily. 'What's the matter?'

'There's a man I . . . met at the dance on Saturday. He's coming here and I don't want to meet him,' Rue faltered.

'Making a nuisance of himself is he?' Tom snarled. 'You stay here. I'll see him off.'

'No, it's not like that, he's a gentleman. I just don't want to see him now.'

'You'll get nowhere running from trouble,' commented the soldier who had won the Military Medal in the desert.

'Please, he's nearly here!' She could see him clearly now. Without the mask his face was as she had guessed, strong rather than conventionally handsome, but conveying the impression of power.

'Go and sit in my bedroom. I'll get rid of him.'

'Thanks Uncle.' She scampered upstairs and sat on the floor by the half open door. She wanted to hear.

There was the sound of a tap on the front door and then her uncle opening it. 'Brigadier Tom Morgan?' His voice was as she remembered it, deep and musical. It gave her an odd thrill to hear it again.

'I am Tom Morgan but I have now retired.'

'My name is John Grey. Martin Fortescue said you might be able to help me.'

There was the smallest of pauses then her uncle said, 'Please come inside Mr Grey.' Rue knew why. Martin Fortescue, now a farmer living some miles away, had served with Tom in the desert and in Italy. Her uncle would never turn away anyone recommended by Martin.

Downstairs there were the sounds of the usual courtesies as the two men settled themselves. Then Tom's voice sounded clearly. 'You mentioned Martin Fortecue?'

'I did,' came the prompt reply. 'When I got your name and rank, I asked myself who I knew who had been in the army and who might know you. I phoned Martin, asked him if he'd vouch for me. If you'd like to phone, Brigadier?'

There was a pause below and then her uncle said carefully, 'I don't think that will be necessary. How may I help you Mr Grey?'

'I am anxious to trace a young lady, height about five feet ten inches, with long auburn hair. She carries herself well and she's beautiful.'

'Why do you think I should know her?'

There was the sound of a soft laugh below. 'On Saturday night she came to a dance in your car. One of the security guards noted the number, and it was easy enough to trace the owner from that.'

'Why do you want to trace her?'

'She came masked and she wasn't the person who had been originally sent the ticket. I would like to know who she is and how she got the ticket.'

Tom said frostily, 'It sounds as if this person was an impostor and has

70

committed some kind of offence. I suggest you return with the police and I'll be more than happy to cooperate with them.'

Upstairs Rue winced. Her uncle had set ideas on certain things and she knew he meant what he said.

'No, it's not like that at all. My interest in the young lady is purely personal. I want to meet her again.'

'Why didn't you arrange that when you saw her last?'

'I very much wanted to, but circumstances beyond my control made it . . . difficult.'

'Does the young lady want to meet you again?'

There was a pause from downstairs and then Rue heard the reflective words: 'Quite possibly not. I had hoped to persuade her to come for dinner.'

'Hmmm,' snorted her uncle. 'In my young day it was the young lady who established the degree of acquaintance. And I can tell you that the person in question will not take kindly to being pursued when she doesn't want it.'

'From the little I've seen of her, I can well believe it,' came the rueful reply. 'However, I think you'll find she agrees that she owes me at least a phone call.' Rue heard the squeak of cushions as the two men got to their feet; her uncle wouldn't sit while his guest stood. 'You obviously don't want to give me her telephone number. I understand that. For the next two days I'm staying in the Sir Charles Dover Hotel. If she could call me there, I'd be most pleased.'

'I'll certainly pass on your message. Now can't I get you a drink? I usually have tea about now.'

'Thank you, but I'm late already and I have other business. If I'm invited, I'd like to call on you again.'

'Quite so Mr Grey.'

'One small thing. Will you please pass on this parcel to the young lady in question?' Rue heard the rustle of paper.

'I'd be pleased to.'

'Then I'll go. It has been a pleasure meeting you Brigadier and I hope we'll meet again.' There was the noise of the door opening and a laughing voice said, 'I'll walk straight to my car so you can tell your niece to come downstairs now. Goodbye.'

'Goodbye Mr Grey,' Tom replied imperturbably, 'I've enjoyed meeting you too.' The door shut and there was the receding sound of footsteps outside. Rue heaved a great sigh. She hadn't realised how she'd been holding her breath.

'I like him,' her uncle remarked as Rue slipped up beside him and slid her arm round his waist. Together they watched as the maroon car drove out of the village. 'Like you said, he's a gentleman.'

'Would you give him a place in your regiment?'

There was a short pause and then, 'There's steel in that young man, he'd make a fine soldier. In wartime, in action he'd be magnificent. But I suspect in peacetime he'd be bored and become a nuisance. He needs to fight.'

Rue blinked; she hadn't thought of John like that. But she could tell what Tom meant. 'What did he leave me?'

'That little packet on the table. Now you open it while I make some tea. All this excitement's getting too much for me.' He gave her a friendly squeeze and went into his kitchen.

Rue took up the packet and looked at it broodingly. It was small, obviously professionally wrapped. She felt that opening it would in some way commit her, that she would be eased into a course of action that might not be entirely what she wanted. She also knew that she just had to know what was inside.

First there was a small leather box with the name of a Scarborough jeweller on top. Inside was tissue paper, and in the tissue paper was — a tiny crystal slipper. Delighted, Rue held it to the light; it shimmered and shot tiny rays of light on her hand. There was also a note. *Cinderella, I'd visit every household in the kingdom, but this one seems to be the most likely. Much love from Prince Charming . . . or Buttons?* She placed the slipper on the table and stared at it, her thoughts a turmoil.

'You'll phone him of course. He deserves that.' Tom returned with the rattle of the tea-tray, and placed it gently on the coffee table.

'It looks like I'll have to. Yes, I'll phone.'

'D'you want to tell me about it? It might help to talk.'

She shook her head slowly. 'I'll tell you later. First I need to get my thoughts in order.'

'When you're ready m'dear. Now, these plants you've brought. I was thinking of an extra flower bed just under my window. Something to catch the judges' eye. What d'you suggest?'

Rue smiled. For the moment the topic of John Grey was obviously closed.

* * *

Through late afternoon and evening Rue worked in her greenhouses like one possessed. Then she tidied her already spotless little bungalow. She had a bath; made herself a complicated meal that she barely noticed eating and finally realised that nothing now could put off the task. By this time the last dinner at the Sir Charles Dover would be long over. For a minute she stared at the crystal slipper. Then she placed it back in its leather case and reached for the phone.

'John Grey speaking.' The musical voice made Rue's already fast beating heart beat faster.

'Mr Grey this is Rue Morgan. You know me better as Pierrette.'

'Or as Cinderella.' The voice was laughing, gently. 'I'm so glad you called Rue. And will you please call me John.'

'How did you know I was upstairs?' Rue asked abruptly. 'And how did you know I was Uncle Tom's niece?'

'There was no great trouble finding that out. When I called at the post office to ask where your uncle lived, Mrs Thwaite there said that your uncle had a visitor — his niece. I described you and she said it was you. Then the floor creaked when you moved upstairs, and your uncle couldn't help looking up.'

'So much for secrecy,' Rue mumbled.

'Why did you run out on me Rue? The lights went up, the dance floor was covered in couples, and right in the middle, there I was like a lemon, smiling at nobody.'

Rue had to giggle. 'Were you embarrassed?'

'I was embarrassed all right. And then in short order I was angry, upset, and finally sad. Why couldn't you tell me who you were?'

'You know I wasn't who you were expecting,' Rue said defensively, 'I thought that explanations would be tedious, and I felt a bit embarrassed myself.'

'Quite. I have a fellow feeling. Incidentally, where is Miss Fiona Blythe-Whitley? If you'd heard the conversation I had with her mother yesterday morning, you'd have been appalled.'

'With any luck she should now be in Los Angeles with her boyfriend.' Rue's curiosity got the better of her. 'What did her mother say?'

'When Fiona didn't return home on Saturday, her mother thought she was with me. She thought it was very naughty of the pair of us, but indicated that there was no harm done that couldn't be put right — apparently by wedding bells. Then I told her that I hadn't seen her, or you, since midnight. She, you, had run away. Mother screamed, 'I'll kill that Peter Hall' and rang off.'

Rue giggled again. 'I seem to have caused more trouble than I realised.'

'It's finished now.' The voice was suddenly serious. 'When can we meet Rue? I've got a meeting early tomorrow evening, but can I take you to dinner afterwards? We've got a lot to talk about.'

This was it. Rue felt a sudden constricting pain in her chest. She'd known this question would be asked, but after hours of thought she hadn't decided on an answer to it. Now there was no time left to think, and the seconds ticked away as she sat speechless.

'Rue? Are you still there? Is everything all right?' The voice was concerned.

'Thank you for a lovely evening on Saturday, John. I'm sorry if you were embarrassed, and you were nice to my uncle, but I don't see any point to our meeting again and I . . . '

'Rue, *please!*'

'Goodbye John.' Rue put down the phone. Then she took the crystal slipper out of its case and sat motionless for an hour, staring at it.

★ ★ ★

Next morning Rue saw John's maroon car in the car park at the Sir Charles Dover Hotel, so she slipped in furtively to leave her vegetables and didn't stay for her customary coffee with Luigi. Then she went back to her market garden and looked for solace, as she always did when she was troubled, in physical work. There were great troughs to be filled with a mixture of sand and peat for her summer flowers. The fact that she probably wouldn't be growing summer flowers she carefully ignored. She needed the work.

To contrast with Rue's grim mood it turned out to be a glorious day; the sun shining in a most unseasonable manner. She opened the end of the greenhouse to let some air in, but even so the temperature rose. Steadily she shovelled, barrowed, spread the mixture in the troughs, getting hotter but deriving some comfort from the physical exertion. After an hour she stopped and rubbed her face with an already damp handkerchief. The sun was at its height. This was Rue's personal empire, no one ever came down here. In the little spare time she had, this was where she sunbathed. After a quick look round she took off her T-shirt and bra. Then she set to work again, feeling happily unconstricted, enjoying the smell of the peat she was moving, and the occasional soft touch of it against her skin.

'Now I know why you're sunburned all over. And I can still see four island moles.'

The voice that came from behind Rue was low and mocking; she recognised it at once. What was John Grey doing here? And how dare he walk through her private land to find her — like this? Rue felt a chaos of emotions seething through her. She was hot, dirty and half naked. She didn't want, or wasn't ready to meet him again. Hadn't she made that clear? If she did meet him again, she wanted it to be on her own terms. Unfortunately he was here, now. Her back was to John; her shirt was on the wall behind him. For some reason anger got the better of embarrassment. She was not going to run out of the greenhouse like some frightened child; that would be undignified and ridiculous. Arms by her side, she stood erect and turned to face him.

He was dressed in a light grey suit, the gold cufflinks, blue silk tie, rose in his buttonhole, making him a picture of male elegance. Rue felt even more enraged. He was leaning casually against one of her troughs, his arms folded. As she walked forward he reached out and handed Rue her shirt. His eyes never left her face.

'It would be a lie to say I'm sorry I caught you like this,' he said calmly, 'but I'm sorry if I caused you any embarrassment.'

Rue slipped into her shirt and her

finger fumbled at the buttons. 'I would have thought you'd have been pleased. After all, I embarrassed you on Saturday night.' She was pleased that her voice sounded self-assured. She didn't feel self-assured.

'I don't want to play games like that Rue. We need to talk.'

'What about?' Rue demanded angrily. 'I thought I made it plain last night. There's no point to our meeting.'

He smiled. 'It's never boring. Tell me what you've got against me. Am I interfering with a current love affair?'

'No,' she admitted reluctantly. 'I did have a sort of boyfriend, but he's gone and I'm glad.'

'Then what? I thought we got on well together.'

To give herself time to think, Rue turned, and started to shovel peat out of her barrow and into a half empty trough. After a moment a muscular arm reached over her shoulder and took the shovel from her. She blinked. John had discarded jacket and tie, rolled up his sleeves and was about to begin shovelling.

'You can't do that,' she squeaked.

'Why not?'

'Well . . . you'll get your suit filthy.'

Deftly he threw peat to the far side of the trough. 'I've got another one or two. Besides, it'll clean.'

'And anyway, don't think you've got to do it just because you're a man. I'm not a weak helpless female you know.'

'I can tell that,' he grinned. 'Now go and fetch me another barrow load while I spread this one. We can work together.'

Speechless, Rue did as he suggested. They remained silent for a few minutes, and she found working as a team quite calming. She asked, 'How did you know where to find me?'

He pointed to his jacket. 'Do you recognise the rose in my buttonhole?'

'No . . . is it one of mine?'

'It certainly is. It was on my table at breakfast; I thought it beautiful and asked the waiter where it came from. When he said that a certain Rue Morgan had delivered it that morning, I knew I had to come.'

Rue felt a small swell of pride. 'If you're interested, I'll show you the other roses later. That is . . .' she realised she had trapped herself.

'I'd very much like to look round,' he said soberly. 'I'm interested in this place — and you.' Rue didn't know what to say. In confusion she bent and seized the handles of the barrow. 'Anyway,' he continued, 'why wouldn't you come to dinner with me?'

'You don't know what Fiona said about you.'

'No I don't,' he mused, 'but I can guess from talking to her mother, and having done business with her father, exactly what our Fiona thought of me. She thought she was to be a sexual sacrificial lamb.'

'That's what you thought too,' Rue pointed out.

For once, John looked a little

uncomfortable. 'Perhaps I was a little ill-mannered to you. If so, I'm sorry.' He turned suddenly. 'Do you think I'm the sort of man to take advantage of someone like Fiona?'

'No,' she said slowly.

'Then why your objection to having dinner with me?'

Rue stood still, trying once again to organise her thoughts, to put into words the formless but very real apprehension she had about him. She knew nothing of him. He was still a man in a mask.

'If the offer's still open I'd love to have dinner with you tonight,' she said.

'Good. I'll pick you up at seven.' His smile was of pure pleasure, there was no feeling of masculine triumph. She was glad she was going.

★ ★ ★

When the troughs were filled, Rue took John to see her flower beds, and then back to the bungalow so he could wash. His once pristine shirt was streaked with soil, and under the faint but expensive smell of his aftershave Rue could now detect the more acrid smell of sweat. She found it exciting, and that excitement she found rather alarming.

While he was in the bathroom she prepared a quick snack, cheese sandwiches and a salad from her garden. As she bent over the fridge her breasts moved under her shirt, and with a blush she ran to her bedroom; she'd completely forgotten to put on her bra. How could I have forgotten, she wondered.

There was a strange ringing noise as she re-entered her little living room and Rue looked around, puzzled. Then John dashed out of the bathroom and grabbed for his coat; in the pocket was a portable telephone. He pulled out the aerial and rapped out his name. She didn't want to eavesdrop so she went back into the tiny kitchen, pulling the door to behind her. It was obviously a business call.

The man who came stern-faced out of her bathroom wasn't the same as the smiling man who'd accepted a towel and walked in. Although she couldn't hear the actual words she could hear the tone of voice; curt, abrupt, with a feeling of authority, even menace to it. Finally the conversation ended, and Rue carried in the little meal.

'Sorry about that,' he apologised, 'but I've got to keep in touch with Head Office.'

'Was it important?' Rue asked.

'Everything's important,' he said distractedly, and Rue could see the effort he made to wrench himself back to her and her world. But he succeeded.

For a while there was a companionable silence as they ate the meal she had prepared. Then, 'I suppose this is a bit unsophisticated for you,' Rue said mischievously.

'Not a lot of hotels I visit would serve it just like this,' he admitted. 'There seems to be a conspiracy against the humble cheese sandwich. It's got to be open, or crustless, or so loaded with goodies that the lot fall into your lap. But I prefer this. And I never get salad like this in London.'

Rue smiled.

* * *

Immediately after the meal he had gone. He told Rue that he still had a couple of calls to make.

'Dressed in a shirt like that?'

He laughed. 'I'll call in at the hotel and change. See you later.'

For the next two hours Rue had pondered what to wear. It wasn't too great a choice; her wardrobe wasn't so extensive. But now she was ready, with that slightly heady feeling of apprehension she hadn't had since she was a teenager.

The fine day had turned into a fine evening, it was warm so Rue had picked out a summer dress. It was simple, with a high neck, no sleeves and blue and white stripes running vertically. Fortunately John was taller than her; it wasn't the dress to wear with a short man. Her brown arms set off the colours. As she sat in front of the mirror, she knew she looked well.

Outside there was the crunch of gravel and the soft purr of a powerful car engine. He had arrived. Grabbing her bag Rue ran outside.

'You look lovely,' he said as he walked round the car, 'though not quite as lovely as when I saw you first this morning.'

'I could blush,' she retorted, 'but instead I'll kick you.' She did.

'Oow,' he yelped. 'I know I deserved it, but it hurt. You're a very physical young woman, Miss Morgan.'

'I am,' she said, and the two looked at each other speculatively.

After a silence he brought a box from behind his back. 'Bringing you flowers is a foolish thing to do. But I tried.'

Rue gasped as she looked through the clear plastic. In the box was a small flower, violently coloured and exotic in shape. It was a Tiger orchid. 'It's beautiful,' she said. 'It makes my flowers . . . '

'Your flowers are just as beautiful. They're different, that's all.'

'That's right,' said Rue.

Driving in the Jaguar was totally different from driving in her van. Whenever Rue exceeded fifty miles an hour the van protested, and there was an impression of great speed and danger. She glanced at the Jaguar's speedometer and was amazed to find that they were cruising at seventy. And the engine was only murmuring.

'I hope we're not going to the Charles Dover for dinner,' she mentioned. 'The manager might find it a bit hard to take, seeing his vegetable supplier in the dining room.'

'You'd look well there,' came the reply. 'We are going somewhere else, but it'll be the Charles Dover's loss.'

The great car drove on to the moors and headed towards the coast. 'Where are we going?' she asked, 'it seems a long way.'

'It's to be a surprise — perhaps for me as well as you. In fact, I'm mixing business with pleasure.'

'I see,' said Rue, rather glumly. She thought that he might have spent the evening concentrating just on her. Things were then made worse as the car phone rang. They parked by the side of the road for him to answer, and to spend ten minutes in hard-voiced conversation about floating stock, which she found entirely incomprehensible, and entirely boring.

'Sorry,' he smiled as they accelerated away. 'But if you're the boss then you're always on call.'

'You're the boss?'

'My firm and my money — so my risk and my responsibility.' It was said rather grimly. Rue was about to ask what he did, then decided she didn't want to know — yet.

They were now dropping down off the moors and headed towards the sea.

Rue fancied she could smell the salt in the air, and after they curled round the top of a hill, she saw it at last, a dark blue stretching to the horizon, with a few tiny breakers. She had always had a childish delight in the sea, and gazed, hardly noticing that the car was slowing down.

'How about here?'

Rue turned to look. They had stopped outside a stone building, obviously once a farm. It had recently been converted; the flowerbeds at the front were new, and there was a freshly laid car park. She thought it showed taste and sensitivity. The sign saying Hood's Bay Restaurant was small and discreet; there were no tacky coloured lights round the door. 'It looks very nice.'

'Come on in, we're expected.'

The entrance hall had the original stone walls, but a bright cherry carpet made it seem warmer. A young receptionist in a black dress greeted John by name and said everything was ready, if they could just come this way. She was a local girl, Rue could tell by the accent, she was also a little nervous. But she led them professionally down a corridor and showed them into a small corner room that overlooked the sea. There was only one table, set for two.

'This is lovely,' Rue exclaimed, 'what a gorgeous view.'

A blush of gratification spread over the girl's face and she bobbed her head. Carefully she settled the two in their chairs. 'Would you care for a drink before dinner?' She took their order and withdrew.

Rue looked round the little room. It too had the original stone walls, but this time the carpet was a deep golden brown. The lights were subdued, and the table was carefully placed so the sea was always in view. On the polished table silver cutlery shone, and there were sparkling glasses.

'Do you like it Rue?' She could tell that, under his apparently careless manner, John had been watching very carefully.

'It's a lovely place. Why have I never heard of it before?'

'It's not been open long. They're trying to make a reputation for themselves. Now, I thought we'd eat first and then I've got some business to attend to.'

'Have you brought me to dinner or a business meeting?' she asked frostily.

Unperturbed, he winked at her. 'Later on I'm going to ask for your invaluable advice. Now, is there anything you really don't like eating?'

She shook her head. 'I'll eat practically anything.'

'Good. Then I suggest we leave it to the chef to serve what he thinks best. Ah, here's our drinks.'

Rue thought that leaving the choice of the meal to the chef was an odd thing to do, but she said nothing. A young waiter entered with two sherries on a silver platter and she accepted hers. John chatted to her companionably about the area; he knew a surprising amount about its history and geology. Then ten minutes later their first course came.

It was a wonderful meal, deftly served by the two waiters, neither of whom could have been out of his teens. First there was a bowl with a crisp pastry topping; when Rue broke it with her spoon there came the rich scent of a clear soup. Then came a devilled crab each, served in its shell with a salad to the side. For the main course there was slices of roast beef, brown on the outside but shading to pink inside, and a selection of seasonal steamed vegetables, fresh, crisp and flavoursome. Finally there were blackcurrant and raspberry ice creams. With the beef came a dark Burgundy, but for the rest of the meal the two drank champagne.

'Would you like the cheeseboard?' the young waiter queried, and both Rue and John shook their heads; to eat any more would be sheer greed.

'No thank you,' John said, 'we'll just have coffee. Would you ask Mr Milner if he'd like to join us?'

'Of course Sir.' The last few plates were snapped up and the waiter left.

'That was one of the best meals I've ever eaten,' Rue said drowsily, 'It was . . .'

'Hush a minute,' John interrupted. 'Wait till Larry joins us. I told you this trip was half business.'

'If I didn't feel so full and contented I'd get annoyed at you,' Rue said reproachfully, 'I don't want to talk business.'

'You will.' At that moment the door opened and a small fat man in an immaculate dinner jacket bustled in. He was followed by two waiters, one carrying a silver coffee tray, the other a tray with brandy and glasses. 'Rue, I'd like you to meet Larry Milner. An old school friend of mine, and the owner of this restaurant. Larry, Rue Morgan.'

'Part owner,' Larry corrected quickly. 'Miss Morgan, so pleased to see you.

Did you enjoy your meal?' His anxiety was obvious.

'I was saying to John that it was one of the best meals I've ever eaten.'

'Ah. I am so glad.' This time his gratification was equally obvious, but Rue noticed that he kept a sharp eye on the two young waiters as they poured and served the coffee and then offered brandy or liqueurs.

The waiters left; the three sat back and sipped their coffee.

'How fresh were the vegetables, Rue?' The question was so brutal that she could hardly believe John had asked it.

'John,' she gasped, 'this is Mr Milner's restaurant!'

'Rue supplies fresh vegetables,' John explained to Larry. 'Her opinion is valuable.'

'Then I would like to hear it. Miss Morgan, tell me honestly, how were they?'

'They were perfect,' Rue snapped angrily, 'obviously bought this morning and cooked exactly right.'

Larry pursed up his mouth and then beamed at Rue. 'I think you're right. In fact I'm certain you're right. And the rest of the service?'

'It was all excellent.'

'Good, good, good, good. Now John, what do you think?'

'I think you were right and I was wrong. The meal and the service couldn't be faulted.'

'So I can . . .'

'If they can get away, fetch them all here.'

'Just for a moment I think. I'll go and see.'

When he'd gone Rue turned to her companion. 'What is going on John? I just don't understand all this.'

He grinned at her amiably. 'I told you that this was part business. You've just taken part in an interview.'

'A what! I . . .' Before she could speak further the door opened and Larry ushered five people in; the receptionist, the two waiters and an equally young boy and girl who, judging by their white dress, were the cooks. All looked a little nervous and when Rue glanced at John she saw why. Although he appeared to be sitting easily and smiling at them, there was an authority about him that was almost tangible.

'When Mr Milner assured me that you were all very competent,' John said quietly, 'quite frankly I wasn't certain. You're all young, I thought you needed time to develop. I was wrong. If you can maintain this evening's standard of excellence, then there's no problem. For tonight's meal, thank you very much, we really enjoyed it. Mr Milner will arrange a bonus. The other thing is — you all now have full time jobs. Thank you.'

Rue could tell by the blushes and the broad smiles how pleased the five were, and there were some muffled thank-yous. But Larry speedily ushered them out and then sat down again with a sigh. 'You've made their day, John.'

'I was genuinely impressed. Can you

keep up the standard?'

Larry indicated that if anyone fell below perfection there'd be trouble.

'Start on the extension then. My solicitors will be in touch about the money later this week.'

'D'you want to go over the costings again?'

'I pay people to do that.' John smiled and poured more coffee.

* * *

A little later they left, and as the Jaguar surged up on to the moors, Rue asked the question that had been puzzling her. 'Come on John, what was that all about?'

'It was about treating you to an excellent meal.'

'You know what I mean,' she yelped, 'tell me or I'll kick you, car or no car!'

He lifted a hand from the wheel in mock surrender. 'Okay, I give in. It's simple. Larry had those five youngsters,

101

trained them as part of a youth scheme. He thought they were really good, but there was no way he could keep them on. He's fully staffed already. The only way to keep them would be to enlarge the restaurant, but he couldn't afford to. I could, I said I would if they were good enough. Producing the meal for us two was his idea of a test.'

'Are you so rich you can afford to do that for a friend?'

'I take risks with money, Rue,' came the grim answer. 'Lending to Larry is a risk, but it's one I've gone into very carefully. I'll make a profit.'

'Is that why you did it?' she persisted.

'Not entirely. Those kids worked hard — but they also had talent. I can give them a chance.'

'John Grey you're an old sentimentalist. You just like helping people.'

'Don't let anyone else know, I'll never hold up my head in the Stock Exchange again.'

Rue smiled but said nothing.

They stopped outside her little bungalow and she told him to put out the car lights and wind down the window. For five minutes they sat in silence, listening to the unobtrusive noises of the night. Then a great shadow swept over the car and headed towards the distant line of trees. Half a minute later there was a mournful hoot.

'That's Ollie my pet owl,' Rue said sleepily. 'He keeps an eye on me.'

'Lucky Ollie.'

'I'm not going to invite you in, not tonight anyway.'

'That's fair enough. After all I'm seeing you tomorrow.'

'Yes please.' He kissed her, lingeringly but gently, his hands stroking the long tresses of her hair.

'Don't get out,' she breathed, 'but phone me tomorrow.'

From his seat he watched until she disappeared in the door. Then, quietly, the great car drove away.

4

Work had to go on. As usual, before daybreak the next morning, Rue was packing her trays with salads, vegetables and flowers, ready for delivery to her three hotels. However, this morning her mood was decidedly different. She sang quietly as she snipped at her salads, and smiled at the hens as she rummaged for eggs. Last night had been wonderful, but Rue felt that the future could be more wonderful still.

For the first time in her life she had met a man whom she thought she could . . . She checked herself. One decision had been made. She wouldn't worry. For the moment she would relax, and let the tide of events wash her where it might. There was still the horror of losing her home and living, but that thought she resolutely pushed to lurk at the back of her mind.

Today would be happy.

It gave her an odd thrill to deliver to the hotel where John was staying, and she scanned the car park for his Jaguar. It wasn't there. For a moment while she was in the kitchen she thought of trying to phone his room, but decided against it. He said he'd get in touch, and Rue knew he would.

For the rest of the morning she worked in the greenhouse nearest the bungalow, the door left open so she could hear if the telephone rang. Normally she didn't bother about the phone when she was working; if anyone wanted her really badly they could keep ringing until she happened to hear.

She decided that if he was free she would invite him to dinner. There was no way she could equal the meal they'd had the night before, but she wanted him to see that she could cook. She also wanted to maintain some of her independence; just because he had more money than her didn't mean that she didn't have anything to offer.

The morning moved on; she worked stolidly and the telephone remained silent. She realised that John was a very busy man and had lots of commitments. He would, of course, ring when he could. For all that, a small sense of disappointment grew slowly inside her.

At five past twelve the phone did ring and, disappointment forgotten, Rue dropped her trowel and rushed inside. 'John, is that you?'

'Who's John?' a familiar but disagreeable voice asked. 'This is Barry. I've been expecting you to ring me.'

So much had happened over the past few days, that for a moment Rue had difficulty almost in remembering who Barry was. It was also unfortunate that he should come on the line when she was hoping for a much more important call. 'Why should I ring you,' she demanded waspishly, 'and what do you want?'

Obviously, this hostile response wasn't the one Barry had been expecting.

Probably decided he'd leave me for a day or two till I realised what I was missing, Rue thought to herself, vindictively. Well isn't he in for a shock?

'I would have thought that what I want is quite obvious,' the voice at the other end of the phone spluttered. 'You're my fiancé remember? I think I do have some rights.'

'Let's get a couple of things clear,' Rue said coldly. 'First, I was never your fiancé. You didn't ask me to marry you; if you had I would have refused. And second, it all finished on Friday.'

'Oh that. I thought you didn't mean it. We were both a bit drunk.'

'You were,' Rue snarled, 'I wasn't.'

'Anyway, I've found you a job. One of my office staff is leaving, you can fill in for her.'

Rue stared at the telephone handpiece and wondered if hammering it against the wall would knock some sense into Barry's head. 'Barry,' she

107

said sweetly, 'I'd rather starve than work for you. I don't want to see you again. I don't want to hear from you. Don't phone, don't write, don't call. Is that clear?' Her voice rose to a shriek.

'You sound as if you mean it,' Barry said incredulously.

'Give me strength,' Rue prayed, and rang off.

Three bedding-out shoots were ruined before Rue took control of her temper. There was no reason to work out her anger on defenceless plants. When the phone rang again ten minutes later, she approached it cautiously. It might be the call she was expecting, or it could be Barry again.

'Good morning. Is this Miss Rue Morgan?' It was a female voice with a definite American accent.

'Rue Morgan speaking.'

'Please hold, I have a call for you.' Rue could hear muttering at the other end of the line, and then a succession of clicks. 'Is that you Rue? It's John here.' Just to hear his voice, so clearly he could be in the room with her, made Rue feel weak, and she sat heavily on the arm of the nearest chair.

'I thought you'd ring before now.' She hadn't intended to sound reproachful, but somehow it came out that way.

He laughed, the low musical sound that she was learning to love. 'I rang as soon as I arrived. Rue, I'm in New York.'

'You're *where?*'

'I'm in New York. Shortly after I got back last night there was a message for me. Something I had to sort out over here. I drove to Manchester and got the overnight plane.'

'Just like that,' Rue said weakly.

'It was only a five hour flight. You can spend that time on a train journey.'

Rue was still struggling to cope with the fact that the man she'd intended to offer to cook dinner for, wasn't in a hotel four miles down the road, but was thousands of miles away in a different continent.

'I was going to invite you to dinner,' she heard herself say.

His voice sounded genuinely regretful. 'I would prefer that to the meal I'm going to get. Rue, I'm flying home on Friday. There's no way I can then come to Yorkshire for a while. Is there any way you can come down to London for the weekend?'

'Where would I stay?' she asked suspiciously.

'Well there are three spare bedrooms in my flat. Or if you wanted, I could put you up in a hotel.'

She thought rapidly. Madge and Harry Allen, the retired couple who were in fact her closest neighbours, took a keen interest in her work and often before had filled in when she had needed a day off. She knew they'd love to look after the smallholding, and the little bit of money she'd pay them would be welcome.

'I can get away for the weekend,' she said, 'but I'll stay with an old girl friend of mine who lives in London.'

'Don't you trust me?' he laughed.

'Do I trust myself?' she retorted, and then blushed, unseen. 'John, I don't know you very well yet. Let's move gently.'

'That's fair enough,' he said soberly. 'Just one thing though. I should come to see you in Yorkshire, but instead you're coming down to see me. Let me at least be responsible for getting you to London.'

'Well, all right,' said Rue, thinking he intended perhaps to pay for her rail ticket.

'That's settled then. Can you be ready and packed say by . . . half two on Friday?'

'Easily,' Rue said, puzzled, 'But I . . .'

'You can indulge me a bit,' he interrupted, 'please, just be there. And Rue?'

'Yes?'

'I'm missing you. Bye.'

For two whole minutes she clutched the buzzing handpiece and then slowly replaced it. One thing about John Grey, he was neither boring nor predictable. As she thought over the past four days she realised they'd been the most hectic of her life. And she had a strong suspicion that things weren't going to quieten down.

★ ★ ★

The rest of the week was quiet. Madge and Harry were very happy to take charge for the weekend. Uncle Tom phoned to say he might be getting somewhere in tracing Rue's landlords. She phoned Melanie Anderson, an old friend from college days who lived in London, and was promptly offered a bed. To be exact she was offered a sleeping bag on the living room settee, but Rue was happy with that. Then, grudgingly, she had to wait.

By two o'clock on Friday she was packed, ready and waiting, dressed in her best — and her only — suit. She had decided that John must have organised a taxi to take her to the station, and was expecting the rattle of a diesel engine. To her surprise there was a knock on the door.

'Miss Morgan? My name's Evans and I'm to take you to London. Is this your baggage Ma'am?'

Rue stared at the middle-aged man in the neat grey uniform who stood on her doorstep. He replaced his peaked cap and reached for her case.

'Yes, that's it,' she said limply.

'Mr Grey sends his apologies for not being able to pick you up himself.'

'You've talked to him?'

'I picked him up at the airport this morning Ma'am. Is there anything else to take?'

She shook her head, and turned to lock the front door. When she turned back she saw how she was to go to London. It was a Rolls-Royce, dark grey in colour and polished till it shone with a dull brilliance. Evans opened the back door for her and showed her the cocktail cabinet, the radio, the intercom so she could speak to him while he was driving.

'Is this . . . Mr Grey's car?'

'Oh yes Ma'am. Well, to be exact, it's the firm's car, but Mr Grey is the firm.'

'I see,' Rue thoughtfully said as she climbed inside. A minute later they were moving down the muddy lane, and then the car silently accelerated along the main road.

Familiar then not so familiar sights passed her window as they drove south, and eventually they were whispering down the motorway. They made hardly any noise but passed nearly everything. Evans was a very good driver, she realised, there were no sudden stops or starts but a continuous smoothness. She flicked through the rack of tapes and selected one she thought appropriate for the occasion, Elgar's *Pomp and Circumstance*. As the rich music flowed round the back of the car she relaxed in the leather upholstery and smiled. This was the way to travel.

It was Friday afternoon, there was more traffic coming out of London than was going in, and Evans skilfully piloted them through the far-reaching suburbs. Eventually they reached the City. It was impressive, but Rue didn't like it much. The great glass skyscrapers seemed to diminish the people she saw, and cast long shadows in the narrow streets below. Only a quick glimpse of familiar St Paul's was reassuring.

The Rolls turned off the road and stopped. Above them was a building she could have just approved of; the sheets of glass were in a particularly pleasant shade of blue, and they were linked by a trellis of bright gold superstructure. A uniformed guard smiled at Evans, but looked closely in the car before pressing the button that lifted a heavy metal barrier. They drove down a curving ramp into the basement.

There was a handful of other cars parked in the basement, a couple of Jaguars, three Porsches and a foreign-looking car which Rue thought was a

Ferrari. I'm glad I don't have to park my van here, she thought to herself. Evans took her to a small glassed-in cubicle where another guard checked a list, and then lifted a phone. 'Someone's coming down for you Ma'am,' he assured her, 'now if I could just have a photograph.' He lifted a large camera. Rue had noticed that everyone she'd met was wearing a plastic badge with name and photograph, soon she was wearing one too. A moment later an incredibly smart young girl was leading her along a thick-carpeted corridor and into a lift.

'Sorry about the security business,' she prattled, 'but we get all sorts of nutters trying to get in. Mr Grey says if he can wear a badge, then we all can.'

'Mr Grey is . . . your boss?' Rue asked, hesitantly.

The girl turned wide black-rimmed eyes on her. 'He's everyone's boss, Miss,' she said, as if finding it incredible that anyone shouldn't know. 'This is his firm and this is his building.'

'Goodness,' Rue said.

She had a quick glimpse of a great room where young men, and women, sat at desks in front of flickering screens, or walked quickly in search of information, and there was the urgent hubbub of low voices. Then they walked into an ante room where an older woman sat behind a desk.

'This is Miss Morgan, Mrs Saunders,' the young girl explained, and then left, with one last surprised look at Rue. Mrs Saunders smiled at Rue and lifted the phone on her desk. 'I have Miss Morgan, Mr Grey.'

A second later a door swept open. Rue had half forgotten the ache that that low voice could produce in her but it came back as strongly as ever. 'Rue . . . come on in. It's good to see you.' He came towards her and kissed her, gently on the cheek. Then he took her hand and led her into his room. Rue had just time to register the instantly concealed surprise on Mrs

Saunders' face; evidently there weren't many people John kissed in his office.

She looked at him. He had taken his jacket off and was dressed in dark trousers and a sparkling white shirt with a black knitted tie. She thought his face was a touch thinner, and there were dark marks under his eyes.

'You look tired,' she said softly, 'too much running from continent to continent.'

He grinned back at her. 'I was tired. But now you're here I feel an awful lot better. Now, can we get you anything? Would you like a drink or something to eat?'

She shook her head. 'I don't want anything just yet.'

'Well, I'm sorry to say this, but I just can't get away for an hour. Do you want to sit here and watch me work, or will I get Mrs Saunders to look after you?'

She grinned. 'Well you helped me spread peat. What can I help you to do?'

He smiled back. 'Come and watch. When you feel ready to start I'll fetch you a shovel.'

The first thing she noticed about his office was the four glowing screens high on one wall, each featuring figures of some sort. As she looked one of them flashed and a new set of figures appeared. Round a small table there were three more men also in shirt-sleeves. John quickly introduced them to Rue, but she could tell by their abstracted smiles that they wanted to get back to what was happening on the screens.

John tried to explain what they were doing, but as the figures on the screens flashed and altered he became more and more engrossed. One of the men had a telephone by him, from time to time he would whisper curt orders down it, to buy or sell. Another sat behind a computer keyboard and his fingers raced over it, calling up information as it was needed. As far as Rue could see they were buying and selling simultaneously in markets throughout the world, apparently trying to buy a large quantity of something without pushing up the price. Before each transaction there was a low-voiced discussion, and Rue was interested to note that although John allowed everyone his say, he took the final decision.

After an hour Mrs Saunders brought coffee in for everyone. Rue's was delicious, but she observed that two of the men barely noticed it had arrived.

Rue felt a growing sense of unreality. The four men in front of her were in another world, watching little electronic pulses on screens as if their lives depended on them. Surely, a set of figures couldn't be that important? She remembered a newsreel film she'd once seen of two chess grand-masters and recognised the intense concentration at once. That was it. This was a giant game.

There was a muttering in front of her and then a small cheer. One of the screens switched off. Men reached for jackets, yawned and stretched. Obviously something had happened. John came over and put his arm round her. 'You've been very patient, but that's it for tonight. It's over now.'

One of the men overheard the remark and called,' Don't believe him. It's only over until his car phone rings.' There was a general laugh, and the three filed out. John leaned over his desk and pressed a button. 'It's Friday Mrs Saunders. Go home now.'

'But Mr Grey . . . ' the box called back.

'Nothing that can't wait,' he said authoritatively, 'I'll see you on Monday.'

'Well thank you. Good night Mr Grey, Miss Morgan.'

John pressed another button and the three remaining screens switched off. For a moment in silence he stood looking at Rue. Then he moved over and took her into his arms.

For a while he just held her, and she could feel the tension seeping from him. Then he kissed her, softly at first and then more urgently, his hand caressing her neck and wrapping itself deep into her hair. Rue gave herself to him, conscious only of the firmness of his muscular body, and her own, softer, against his. After what seemed like an age he broke away. 'You don't know how I've missed you, Rue.'

'I do,' she muttered hoarsely. ' 'Cos I've felt the same way.'

He looked at her in silence for a few moments more, then took her hand and led her out of the building.

* * *

'I thought you'd like the view,' John said cheerfully, 'I know it's not quite up to the North Sea, but it's the best I can do. Look, there's the Houses of Parliament.'

Reluctantly she turned away from the window. They were in a restaurant high above London and far below them the whole of the city was revealed like a

122

glittering fairyland.

'It's fantastic,' she said. 'But you're right. It's not quite up to the North Sea. How are you?'

He frowned slightly at her bald question. 'I'm fine, I guess. Why do you ask that?'

'You look tired, and you must be. Practically every time I see you you're working. Last Tuesday, after a lovely evening with you, all I wanted to do was go to sleep. You managed to get to America. How d'you do it?'

'I concentrate,' he smiled. 'I won't say I don't enjoy it, I do. But to stay on top in this business you've got to work all the time.'

'Can you keep it up indefinitely?'

'I have done so far. But everyone burns out sometime. There are no old men in this business.'

She shivered at these bleak words. 'Why d'you carry on then?'

He thought for quite a while before answering. 'People must do what

123

they're best at. They owe it to themselves.'

'And you're best at . . . ?'

'I've earned a great deal of money. But I hope I have other talents. Some day soon I intend . . . '

'My word it's John Grey! And with a most beautiful young lady too!'

'Arthur! I thought you were in Hong-Kong.'

'Returned today. We must have dinner soon.'

Rue was quickly introduced to a tall white-haired gentleman, well into his seventies but with a very youthful gleam in his eye. In spite of John pressing, he would not join them. 'You two don't want the company of an old feller like me. Besides, brought a crowd back with me from Hong Kong. Got to show 'em the sights.' With a friendly wave he went to his table.

'He seems a pleasant man,' Rue ventured.

John smiled. 'He is. I worked for him when I first came to the city. I learned a lot.' He paused a moment, then, 'You know the fight we were having this afternoon — buying and selling shares.'

'Yes,' she said carefully.

'Well Arthur there could have told us what we were trying to find out. And we all could have made a lot of money — even him.'

'You couldn't ask him?' Rue asked, surprised.

'The city runs on trust. It would be improper for him to tell me and I wouldn't ask him. We all have to play by the rules.' He smiled at her mystified expression. 'Now what would you like to eat?'

She took one look at the menu, a long list of exotic sounding French dishes and gave up. 'Just for once you order for me. But this will be the last time you do.'

He beckoned the waiter.

★ ★ ★

At ten he drove her back to his flat for coffee. He lived on the top floor of an older block of apartments overlooking Regent's Park.

'My old headmistress told me I couldn't tell the difference between intellectual curiosity and nosiness,' she said to him as they purred upwards in the lift, 'but I want to see where you live. You can learn a lot about a person from the way he organises his home.'

'I hope my cleaning firm have dusted everything and made the beds.'

'Oh, I shan't be going in the bedrooms,' she said primly, and then burst out laughing.

'What d'you want to learn about me?'

'Today is only Friday, and I met you for the first time last Saturday. I don't really know you very well.'

'I don't know you very well either,' she said soberly, 'but I want to find out.' For a moment he looked at her, and then his voice changed. 'Now. See what guilty secrets my flat reveals.'

From his pocket he took a bunch of keys, and, using two of them, unlocked the door. Then he used a third to switch off his alarm system. Rue thought of her own front door; a hefty push would break it open, but she said nothing.

Once inside she realised why he was so security conscious. The flat itself looked just as she had half guessed, apart from a hi-tech kitchen John had furnished it with antiques. The living room had a hardwood floor with a Persian rug covering it that was sheer beauty. The dining room had Regency chairs, table and sideboard. And every available wall surface was covered with paintings, from a tiny but bright depiction of angels that she decided was medieval, to a lurid splash of colour, representing apparently nothing, that had to be modern. Delighted, she moved from one to the other while John went into the kitchen to make coffee.

'You're an art lover,' she called out to him.

A voice came back from the kitchen.

'Lover is the right word. There's not one painting there that I bought because it was an investment. Each one I wanted because it was beautiful.'

'It must be nice to be able to buy so many lovely things,' she said wistfully, realising again that having a lot of money could buy the good things in life.

John appeared with a tray. 'They shouldn't be here just for me and my guests,' he commented. 'Other people should be able to see them. Perhaps one day . . . ' He said nothing more, but led her out on to the balcony.

They sat side by side on a bench, the coffee in front of them and the ever present murmur of London traffic in their ears. John put his arm round her and she rested her head on his shoulder. His lips moved over her hair. 'Are you really going to sleep at your friend's tonight?' he asked gently.

She put her arm further round him and squeezed. 'Do you really want me to stay? Go on, be honest.'

He laughed. 'You know me too well already. A lot of me desperately wants you to stay. The sensible part tells me not to rush. We've got time ahead of us.'

'That's true. Come on, you're tired. I don't know what state you'll be in tomorrow morning, you must be jet-lagged. I'll take a taxi to Melanie's and you go to bed.'

'You will not take a taxi! But I'll take you now.'

He said little as they drove through the now quieter traffic, but drove one-handed, holding her right hand with his left. She gazed at his face, illuminated by the street lights outside. Inside her, a turmoil of emotion welled, so strong that words could not compass it, so strong that tears glittered in the sides of her eyes. She knew, with an utter feeling of rightness, that she was in love.

5

Eventually the car pulled up outside a large, obviously converted Victorian house in north London. Melanie's muffled voice screamed from the intercom, 'Rue! at last! Just push the door and come up.' The automatic door opened with a rattle and Rue walked inside.

Like John's flat, Melanie's was on the top floor. Unlike his, it had no lift. Rue had puffed up three flights before Melanie, running down, met her, shouting greetings all the way. She grabbed Rue and hugged her.

'Rue Morgan, you look great! There's a sparkle in your eye — you're up to something!'

'What could I be up to?' Rue protested. 'All I do is work.'

'I don't know yet, but watch me find out! Come on inside, we've got hours of gossip to catch up on.'

Melanie and Rue had been friends at College. They had shared a room and often everything else they had: clothes, make-up, money, food and even boyfriends. Melanie had been Rue's greatest comfort when her father died. They both regretted seeing so little of each other since, but Melanie was pursuing a precarious career designing and making clothes and was seldom able to get away.

Rue looked at her friend affectionately. Melanie was big-boned, dieting could never do anything much for her. So proudly she made the most of herself, wearing eye-catching colours and dramatic styles. Tonight she was dressed in a bright scarlet track suit.

'Who's this man then?' she demanded as she grabbed Rue's bag and led her upstairs. 'If he's rich and you're going to marry him, then I want to design your wedding dress. Make my name and fortune. And I'll lose a stone and whip myself something up so I can be chief bridesmaid and marry his best friend.'

'I've only known him a week,' Rue objected, 'don't hurry me.'

'Hmmm. If you'll abandon your plants for a weekend — then you're getting serious. I only hope he is. Welcome to my simple home!'

Melanie's attic flat was an extension of her personality. There was one main room, with swatches of cloth and half finished garments all over it. The walls were covered with posters and sketches Melanie had made. Just to look at it made Rue feel young again, as if she was still a student.

'D'you want anything to eat or a bath perhaps?' Melanie asked solicitously.

Suddenly Rue felt tired. It had been an exciting but an exhausting half day, and she needed to get her thoughts in order. 'I'd love a bath,' she said, 'I just need to relax. And then a cup of cocoa and bed.'

'You're not going to sleep until you've talked to me for at least an

132

hour,' Melanie called, 'but the rest is fine.' She disappeared and Rue heard the rattle of a filling bath.

It felt just like old times. Rue stretched out on the settee in Melanie's promised sleeping bag: Melanie lying, as she'd always loved doing, full length on the hearth rug. Each clutched a large mug of cocoa made (another student memory) with condensed milk.

' . . . so he knows how I feel about him. And I think he feels the same way about me. It's just that things are going so fast.' Rue had just told Melanie all about John — the meeting with Fiona, the masked ball, the dinner and the trip to America, the invitation to London. Talking about the affair made it seem more real; she realised that not having a close friend to confide in made her too introverted.

'And he's good-looking?' Melanie demanded.

'Gorgeous,' Rue said with relish. 'A bit older than me, but he keeps fit.'

'And he's rich as well. How rich?'

This was something Rue still had difficulty in coming to terms with. She tried to avoid thinking about John's money, but it had to be faced. 'I'd say he was a millionaire,' she muttered, 'but I suspect he might be a millionaire several times over.'

'So what's he doing chasing a country girl with dirt under her finger nails?'

Rue darted a jaundiced look at her friend. 'Perhaps he has a taste for the simple things in life. Ow!'

Melanie, after poking Rue in the ribs with her outstretched finger, lay back again with an expression of pleasure. 'Don't come it with me Chummy, I *know* you. You're worried about the money aren't you?'

Rue murmured, 'Yes.'

'A man like you've described could have his pick of women. Why has he picked you?'

'I've wondered a lot about that. I think he loves me.' Rue wriggled round and looked. Her friend was unusually serious-faced. 'You don't like him do you?'

'I've never met him, but from what you've said about him I think he's wonderful. I'm just a bit suspicious of all men at the moment. And I don't want my old pal getting hurt.' She paused a moment. 'You're not upset by my cynical views are you?'

'No. There's nothing you've said that I haven't thought. It's good that you've put things into words.'

'You deserve a good man,' Melanie said gruffly.

'I might have one. Anyway, let's talk about your love life now.' Rue couldn't help it. She yawned, and then felt annoyed when she heard Melanie chuckle.

'At the moment I'm between men. However, I refuse to cheat the chemist by boring you to sleep. We'll talk tomorrow. Night love.' Before Rue could stop her, she had gone.

* * *

Next morning they woke late, and then spent a gratifying idle couple of hours drinking coffee, reminiscing and looking over the clothes Melanie was currently making. By tacit consent, John wasn't mentioned. Eventually Rue gave a squeak, 'Look at the time! And I'm not even dressed.'

'Plenty of time,' Melanie said carelessly. 'The bathroom's all yours. He'll be hours yet.'

She was wrong. The moment the bathroom door shut, the downstairs bell rang. Melanie rushed round, grabbing empty mugs and throwing strewn clothes where they couldn't be seen. 'Hell, that'll be him,' she screamed. 'What shall I do? I'm just in my dressing gown.'

'You'll have to let him in,' a desperately muffled voice came back, 'I'm just in my knickers.'

'You always get me into trouble, Rue Morgan.'

136

Melanie called hello down the intercom; with any luck it might be someone else.

'My name is John Grey,' she heard a voice say, 'I'm calling for Miss Morgan.'

'Come on up. Top floor.' Gloomily Melanie looked around her. She was suspicious of this man. Now he was going to be able to laugh at her. In an incredibly short time there was a tap on the door.

'Miss Melanie Anderson isn't it? I'm John Grey.'

'Er, come in,' Melanie gurgled, open-mouthed at the excessively beautiful man in front of her.

He stepped inside. 'It's good of you to put Rue up when she's spending so much time with me. Will you have these flowers as a peace offering?'

Melanie looked at the bunch of red, pink and white roses. Her artist's eye responded to them at once. 'How lovely . . . thank you.' She waved ineffectually in the general direction of the settee.

'Er please sit down. I'll just put these in water.'

She returned from the kitchen to find him studying her drawings. 'Have you time for a coffee, before you go out?' she asked. 'Rue won't be long but . . .'

'I'd love one,' came the prompt reply. 'And can you shout through the keyhole to Rue, and tell her not to move so fast. We've got all afternoon.'

'You've heard the frantic bumps from the bathroom?'

He grinned. 'I hate having to wash and dress in a hurry. These things should be taken gently.'

I like him, Melanie thought to herself in the kitchen. He's everything she said he was, and more. I only hope he's good for her. She carried his coffee through.

'John! sorry I wasn't ready but we had a 'girls together' morning.' Rue burst out of the bathroom, eyes bright with delight.

'You were well worth waiting for,' he

said gently, and Melanie felt a certain easing of tension; he meant it, he was in love she'd swear.

'Where are we going?'

'Surprise time. But one thing first.' He turned to Melanie. 'I do feel guilty about keeping Rue from you. Will you have dinner with us tonight? If you have a partner, do please bring him.'

Melanie did something she hadn't done in years, she blushed, with delight. 'I er, haven't got a boyfriend right now, so I'd just be in the way. You two go on your own.'

'John, she wants to come but she's being polite. Tell her she's got to come.' Rue's voice echoed across the room.

John grinned. 'Looks like your mind's being made up for you. Will half past six be all right?'

'I'd love to come,' Melanie agreed, happily. 'And half past six is fine.'

* * *

139

'Travelling round central London is murder,' he said as they trundled down a hill in a taxi, 'and parking's even worse. I usually travel by underground or if I can't walk I have been known to travel by bike.'

Rue looked at him astonished. 'Bike? Chief executive chaining his transport to the railings. Don't all the minions laugh at you?'

'Certainly not,' he said sniffily. 'Besides, I always get the receptionist to do the chaining. My transport gets parked for me.'

As she shrieked with laughter at the thought, the slowly moving taxi came to a gentle halt. She looked out of the window to see a morass of traffic: buses, cars, taxis, lorries, all stuck fast. Suddenly a cyclist flashed past her window, one of the many message deliverers, dressed in crash hat and bright crimson lycra shorts. He weaved his way through the stationary vehicles to reach the front of the queue.

'And I wear pin-striped lycra shorts,'

John added and Rue laughed again. She was enjoying herself.

And she and Melanie had decided years ago that if you could share a sense of humour with a man, then you'd probably get on in other ways.

The taxi cautiously edged forward another few feet. 'Where are we going?' she asked. 'I know we're heading for the centre of town, but where specially?'

'Where would you like to go, Rue? I've not known you long, I don't really know all your likes and dislikes. We can have a long lunch, or we can look at the shops or there's museums . . . art galleries . . . all the tourist things.'

'Are we going anywhere near Trafalgar Square?'

'You want to feed the pigeons!'

'I hate pigeons,' Rue snarled. 'They eat all my seedlings. No, I know it's a bit touristy, but I'd really like to go to the National Portrait Gallery. I've never been and I've always wanted to.'

When he made no reply she glanced

at him; he was looking at her with a most peculiar expression. 'Of course, if you don't want to, we can do something else,' she added quickly.

He leaned over and kissed her quickly on the cheek. 'No Rue. The Portrait gallery suits me fine. In fact it fits in very well with what we're doing later.' But he wouldn't add to this remark.

Compared with the National Gallery next door, the Portrait Gallery seemed quite small and welcoming. Rue had always loved paintings, and paintings of people most of all. Slowly she moved from picture to picture, entranced by her knowledge of who the people were, and how the painter had tried to capture the spirit as well as the appearance of his sitters. As a young girl she had read all the Brontë novels, and stood enthralled in front of the famous picture of the three of them, finding their appearance as enigmatic as their novels.

'How many times have you read

Wuthering Heights?' came the whispered question.

'I've lost count,' she replied abstractedly, 'it must be dozens.' Realisation suddenly hit her. 'How did you know that was my favourite book?'

He waved towards the arrayed portraits. 'Peoples' appearance tells you something about them. You sometimes have that wild look that makes me think of the northern moors. Emily Brontë would have approved of you.'

Rue turned to study him for a moment, tall lean and urbane. 'You're not an Emily Brontë fan,' she said positively. 'She's who you read.' She pointed to a picture a little distance away.

He looked and nodded. 'Jane Austen. You're right . . . but why do you think so?'

'I met you first at a masked ball. There's always something a bit hidden about you, you keep your feelings controlled. Jane Austen would have liked that.'

'But do you?' he teased.

'It's not me — but I'm working on it.'

He put an arm around her shoulder. 'Keep trying. And I'll see if I can alter too.' She found this comforting.

When they were tired of standing so much they had a quick coffee and a roll and then, at Rue's suggestion, set off to walk rather than take the underground or a taxi. John still wouldn't tell her where they were going, merely that they would call on a friend of his who lived in Bloomsbury. The weather was fine, noticeably warmer than the north, and Rue enjoyed the cosmopolitan crowds and the very different shops. She lingered outside Foyle's bookshop, but knew that once inside she'd never get out. John watched her silent inward struggle, a smile on his face.

'Do you know what next Wednesday is?' he asked, piloting her expertly across the road.

She shook her head.

'It's my birthday. I won't tell you

how old I am . . . but what are you going to get me for a present?'

'What d'you give the man who has everything,' she parried, 'another tie? Spare pair of socks?'

He winced. 'Don't even say that as a joke. No, you've got something I want that only you can give.'

She elbowed him hard in the side. 'And I'm hanging on to it John Grey. It certainly won't be a birthday present!'

'You *have* got a dirty mind Rue Morgan. What would Emily Brontë say? This is something quite different?'

'Flowers? Fresh vegetables?'

'Both very nice, but it's neither of them.'

'Do you know you're a very irritating man sometimes,' she muttered, but he would say no more.

They had now crossed New Oxford Street and he led her behind one of the great Georgian terraces and into a mews which was barred to traffic. They crossed the cobbled street and passed small, elegant and obviously expensive shops; a handbag and silk scarf shop, a milliners and an antiquarian bookshop. John led her into the shop at the end of the street. In the window was a bunch of flowers and a single picture on an easel; she caught a glimpse of a head and shoulders in dark heavy colours. The glass door of the shop carried the name 'Harriet Brand' in gold.

Inside the shop was a miniature art gallery. On the white walls there were pictures, each with a small light above it. By the door a large blond young man sat at a desk, he smiled and nodded when John told him that they would look round for a moment.

'See what you think,' John whispered to her. 'Are they as good as the paintings we've just seen?'

Rue moved down the wall, studying the pictures. All were portraits of some kind; of face alone, of head and shoulders, of a family group. There were four or five nudes, posed to look sensual but not grossly sexual. Rue was fascinated; somehow the character of each subject stood out in the portrait. She felt she knew which people she'd like to meet, who would be fun to be with, who would be wilful, who would be a crashing bore. She paused in front of one picture, a man whose basic unpleasantness stood out in the twist of the mouth and the screwed up malevolent eyes.

'Is that what he's really like?' she asked John who was just behind her. 'That's a brilliant picture of someone who's really awful.'

'It's very accurate,' John replied. 'He is awful. The interesting thing is, he really likes the picture. Wants another one done for his boardroom.'

'Good Lord.' Rue was baffled.

John spoke to the blond young man who spoke quietly into a telephone on his desk and then nodded, 'If you'll go upstairs, sir.' John took her arm and led her through a door at the back of the gallery and then up a circular staircase. 'D'you like the paintings?'

'I think they're brilliant,' she confessed,

'I've never seen character shown so well in a picture.'

'Good. You can get me one for my birthday.'

'John! I couldn't even afford the frame, never mind the picture.'

'We'll ask the artist then if she'll do one cheaply.'

He pushed open a door and they entered a vast, light filled studio that was so much a muddle it made Melanie's flat look tidy. There were odd pieces of furniture, a vast gilt mirror, piles of old books. On every surface there were drips of paint or jam-jars full of brushes. There was an exciting smell, half coffee half turpentine and the air jangled with the sound of loud pop music from a portable radio. It was a complete contrast to the serenity of the gallery below.

'Look who I've brought, Harriet,' John bellowed, 'tell me what you think.'

There was a click and sudden silence.

From behind a large easel a woman stepped and frowned fiercely at the two of them. Rue blinked. The woman was small, with her hair tied tightly in a knot. She was dressed in a shapeless smock, with splurges of paint across the front and her feet were bare. Rue guessed her age at about fifty.

'Harriet, this is the girl I told you about — Rue Morgan.'

'Hmmm. Take all those pins out of your hair girl, and I'll fetch you some coffee.' The small figure disappeared and Rue turned to John, who merely grinned and shrugged. Rue had thought her hair wasn't too bad. It was certainly neat. 'What shall I do?' she hissed at John.

'I love your hair long. Why not take it down, as you were asked?'

'Funny way of asking,' she muttered, but did it anyway. Everyone knew that artists were eccentric.

Harriet reappeared with a tray holding three mugs and a giant silver coffee pot. The coffee she poured was strong and black, no milk was offered. Rue sipped a little, winced and realised that she liked it.

'Come over here,' Harriet ordered and led Rue to a tall stool in the middle of the only clear space in the room. She took off Rue's coat, sat her on the stool and then walked round, pulling her long hair this way and that, holding it out and letting it drop where it would. Then she put a finger under Rue's chin and moved her head gently, staring at Rue's face with eyes that were such a dark blue as to be almost black.

'Yes,' she muttered to herself, 'yes indeed. I think we can make something of you.'

Rue was getting a bit tired of this. 'I'm so glad,' she said tartly, and Harriet grinned.

'I like a bit of spirit,' she said, 'so let's go and talk business. John! When d'you want me to start?'

'Just a minute,' Rue put in, 'it seems like decisions are being made about me without me knowing. What's going on?'

'It's my birthday present,' John said, 'you promised me one.'

'I can't afford one of these pictures!'

'I'll pay for it and I'll own it. The present will be you sitting for it.'

Rue didn't quite know what to say. Harriet Brand was obviously an expert painter, and she felt a sense of excitement at being a model. 'I'd love to,' she said slowly, 'but really, I couldn't spare the time to come down to London. I've got my work.'

'You live near York don't you?' Harriet put in.

Rue nodded. 'It's about an hour away.'

'That's fine then. Next week I'm moving up there for three months. Got an exhibition and I'm doing a bit of teaching and one or two local portraits. You can be the first.'

'Is that all right Rue?' John asked anxiously.

'Well yes.' She felt that things were

moving just a little quickly, but was surprised to realise she didn't mind.

'Good. Harriet, you get in touch with Rue and sort out times. Meanwhile . . . here's a cheque.'

Harriet took the small piece of blue paper, and only her slightly uplifted eyebrows gave Rue any inkling of what she was thinking.

'Don't you want to tell me what sort of picture I'm to paint?' she asked John. 'For this much money most sitters think they're entitled to some kind of say in the matter.'

'I'll bet they don't get it.' John leaned forward and stroked Harriet's cheek. 'You've seen my paintings, Harriet. I want Rue's picture in the centre, the most beautiful thing I have.'

'Right next to that blotchy American thing that looks like a fried egg gone wrong,' Rue suggested.

'That cost me twenty thousand pounds,' John said, scandalised.

'I'm looking forward to painting you,' Harriet said.

★ ★ ★

The rest of the weekend was a happy dream for Rue. She seemed to be more alive than she'd been in years. Only now did she realise that she needed much more than her life on the smallholding, she needed companionship, someone to try her sharp wit on. She knew she also needed love, but she was a little afraid of rushing. John seemed to guess this and didn't push her.

He dropped Rue at Melanie's flat and then called back an hour later for the two girls. Melanie had been uncharacteristically shy and it took all Rue's powers to persuade her to come out with them. However, once they were sitting together on a café terrace overlooking the river, the conversation flowed and bubbled and all three enjoyed themselves. After a long relaxed meal Melanie shyly suggested they might all like to come back to her flat for a nightcap and was pleased and amazed when John said he'd love cocoa with condensed milk — but should he bring some champagne as well?

'You've got a winner there,' she mumbled to Rue, just before the two went to sleep.

'You like him? You don't think he . . . ?'

But Melanie was already asleep.

Next morning John called and took her up the river on a cruise. Like two typical tourists they wandered round Hampton Court, enjoying the sun and the sense of freedom. After a while they walked on the river bank. John had brought his portable telephone, but only once was there a call for him, and Rue tried not to listen to the peremptory tones, the curt orders and the cold decisions. Then he lay on the grass by her side and the two listened to the Thames lapping below.

'Don't you ever get fed up with that machine?' she asked drowsily.

He shrugged. 'Often. But it's part of the job and I've got to do the job as

154

well as I can. Someday Rue I'll . . . '

'You'll give it up?'

'I've got vague plans. Come on, if you must travel by train we'd better get you back to the flat.'

'I wish I could stay,' she said wistfully.

He winked. 'It looks like the fairy godmother is falling down on the job.'

Rue had firmly refused to be taken back home by car. There was an excellent train; she'd take that. After an argument there was a compromise, she could travel by train but he'd pay for the ticket.

He waited outside in a taxi while she panted upstairs to pick her bag up from Melanie's flat. Melanie was out, she'd claimed she had work to do, whether this was true or Melanie being tactful Rue didn't know.

Using her borrowed key Rue let herself into the empty flat. There was a large sheet of paper pinned to the wall in front of her. 'Rue — urgent — Ring your uncle.' Fearfully she grabbed the phone, her hands shaking. It wasn't like her uncle to panic. Only something serious would have caused him to get in touch like this.

'Are you all right?' she babbled when she heard his firm tones on the line. 'You're not ill?'

'I'm perfectly well and there's nothing wrong with the smallholding.'

Rue was instantly relieved, but she could detect a guarded, rather a sad note in her uncle's voice. 'Well, what's the matter then? You had me worried.'

There was a pause, then her uncle spoke to her in the clipped tones that she knew concealed real feeling. 'I've had a couple of friends trying to find out exactly who is buying your land. I know now.'

For some reason Rue just didn't want to hear what was coming next. 'Go on,' she said.

'It's all very cleverly organised through holding companies abroad and at home. A firm called Capital, Venture and Trust ultimately own the land. And that firm is largely owned by your friend, John Grey.'

Rue felt her world, her dreams of happiness, collapse around her. 'Perhaps he just doesn't know!' she said weakly.

'I thought of that. He gave the order to foreclose. He knows all right.' After a moment the old man said, concerned, 'Are you all right Rue? I can guess what a shock this must be.'

'I'm all right,' Rue lied, and bit her lip till the taste of blood tingled on her tongue. 'I'll see you when I come back. Bye.' She rang off.

For a minute she leaned against the wall, shoulders shaking with great silent sobs. Then she walked to the bathroom and dipped her face into a basin full of cold water. When she walked down those stairs she was going to be in command. It took another five minutes, but when she finally picked up her bag, and slammed the flat door behind her, no one could tell from the cold hard face that she had been weeping.

Once again John was talking into his portable phone when she reached the cab, so she was able to get inside before he could get out to open the door for her. The cab lurched forward towards the station.

' . . . so they're agreeable. That's great news. Pay them the money at once. Bye.' He snapped the phone shut with a decisive click. 'I've got some good news for you Rue — at least, I hope it's good news.'

'Go on,' Rue said flatly from the darkened corner of the cab.

'You can stay longer — we can be together all week. That was one of my men. He's just been to see your neighbours — the Allens — who are looking after the smallholding. He's offered them double what you pay them to work for the rest of the week. They jumped at it.'

'They certainly need the money,' Rue agreed. 'They're both over seventy and the work might kill them — but it would be nice for them to die rich.'

There was silence for a moment, broken only by the click as John leaned forward and shut the window dividing them from the driver. 'That's unfair, and you know it,' he said gently. 'When you went upstairs you wanted to stay. Now you don't. What happened to make you change your mind?'

'Are you in charge of the company that's forcing me out of my land?' The question lashed at him, but Rue desperately, hopelessly, wanted him to deny it.

'Ah. You've heard. I bet your uncle found out.' There was reluctant admiration in the voice.

'Will you answer my question!'

'Rue, it's not as simple as you make out. I run the company but it's not my money.'

'But you are throwing me out.'

He sighed and then bleakly said — 'Yes.'

'I know I was nothing to you when you first decided — how could I have been? But why didn't you tell me later?'

'Would you still have gone out with me if I had?'

'Never,' Rue snarled. 'But I would have respected you more.'

He flinched as if she had struck him. 'I know you're upset,' he said, 'and I sympathise why. I've tried to tell you several times but somehow I couldn't bring myself to. You must believe, it's the first confrontation I've ever backed away from. But I couldn't bear to make you unhappy, and so I let things ride.'

'Don't let your City friends hear you say that,' she said bitterly, 'they'll think you're losing your touch.'

She paused for just a second and then went on, 'Without the money you might be quite a nice man. But you don't own the money. It owns you.'

'Rue, try to listen to me. One of the reasons I wanted you to stay was so we could get this sorted out. You just don't understand.'

The taxi had gently pulled up in front of the station and Rue grasped her bag and prepared to stand, throwing off John's restraining hand. 'I understand enough. Goodbye John. I don't ever want to see you again.'

He grabbed her almost brutally and pushed her back into the seat. 'Rue you can't just deny what we mean to each other. You feel it as much as I do.'

'I can deny it. I love you with all my heart John. But with my brain I despise you and all you stand for. Now let me go.'

Instantly he released her and Rue stepped on to the pavement. Then she turned to the white-faced figure staring at her and said, 'Don't call, don't write, and especially don't have one of your nasty little men come to see me. If there's ever any need I'll get in touch. But I'm sure there won't be. Now is that perfectly clear?'

'Yes, you've made your position quite clear Rue. I shall never bother you again.' Rue realised that the bleak

161

figure speaking to her had regained his confidence and some tiny corner of her mind knew she was going to regret what she had done. She took her bag and walked proudly into the station concourse, grimly determined not to look back. When she knew she couldn't be seen she turned. The taxi had gone. Rue bought a ticket, the Sunday papers and boarded her almost empty train.

6

On the train going north Rue stared steadfastly but unseeingly out of the window, ignoring the plaintive attempts of the little man opposite her to start a conversation. The taxi driver who drove her home from the station was the father of an old acquaintance and she had to be polite to him, but she pleaded a headache. When she finally got to her bungalow, wanting nothing more than solitude to sob her heart out, she found the Allens still working there, genuinely concerned about her unexpected return and her welfare.

'Don't bother about the work,' Rue said, 'but keep the money. I was going to stay away all week but I changed my mind.'

Harry Allen shook his head. 'We'll not take payment for work we haven't done. I'll bring the money round in the morning and perhaps you'll send it back.'

Rue just caught the glance he exchanged with his wife, and realised that they had been counting on the unexpected windfall. 'Well, there's a lot of calls I've got to make,' she invented hurriedly, 'so if you don't mind carrying on I'd be most grateful . . .'

'We'd like that, lass.'

Rue had been exaggerating when she told John that the extra work might kill the old couple, she knew they were still both perfectly fit. Ordinarily she liked their company, but now all she wanted was to be alone. They had a cup of tea together, talked about the work of the smallholding and then the Allens left.

When they had gone Rue discovered that she was sorry. Their company had forced her to be polite, to think of others and not herself. But now she was home and could not help but think of her own problems. All there was in front of her was a void — a future without enjoyment, without prospect, without hope. She lay sleepless in bed, unable to repel the images and memories of John that floated through her mind.

* * *

Late on Tuesday evening the phone rang. Rue looked at it cautiously. Not many people would telephone her this late at night.

'Rue Morgan?' a harsh, vaguely familiar voice rasped down the line. 'This is Harriet Brand. You're going to sit for me.'

Recollections of a perfect day in London flashed back even more vividly than before, and tears sprang to Rue's eyes. She hadn't been expecting this.

'Are you there?' the voice continued, and Rue managed to mumble that Harriet had surprised her, she wasn't expected until next week.

'Ah. Had a bit of luck. My studio was ready earlier than I thought, and here I am in York, ready to work and no sitters laid on. I wondered if you

165

could come this week.'

Rue gritted her teeth and said what had to be said. 'Miss Brand, John Grey and I won't be seeing each other again. I doubt he'll want a picture of me.'

'Hmmm! Well he's certainly not cancelled his cheque, and if I know him he won't. Are you saying you won't sit for me? I don't want to send the money back.'

Rue thought that John's money seemed to be having a malevolent influence, almost a life of its own. 'I'd like to sit for you Miss Brand. At the moment I've nothing much on myself.'

'Good. Get here as early as you like tomorrow morning. Bring some of your favourite clothes — we'll decide what you're to wear when you get here. I'm looking forward to it.' Harriet gave careful directions and rang off.

For a minute Rue sat, wondering if she was punishing herself by hanging on in this way to her short time with John. Then she decided that she liked

Harriet Brand, she had nothing much to do with her time and she quite liked the idea of being an artist's model. She went and opened her wardrobe door.

The first thing that she saw was, of course, the long blue dress she'd worn to the masked ball, and for a moment she thought of asking Harriet to paint her in her mask. Then she realised it would be too painful. Turning away from the dress she rummaged through wardrobe and drawers, and assembled a case full of clothes. When she finally went to bed her usual haunting memories were this time of the masked ball.

★ ★ ★

'Come in. Take your coat off, unpin that hair and I'll fetch the coffee.' Harriet obviously didn't believe in spending too much time on the niceties of polite conversation. As Rue did as she was told, she looked round the new studio. Compared with the one in

167

London it was comparatively tidy, but there were already signs that it wouldn't stay that way for long.

'Bit characterless isn't it,' Harriet called cheerfully, appearing with the coffee tray, 'but I'm working on it. Now, my name's Harriet not Miss Brand, and we'll start painting by sitting here and gossiping. You can spend an hour or so telling me about yourself.'

'It's a funny way to paint,' Rue said, confused.

'It's my way, and it must work 'cos I get very well paid. Tell me where you were at school.'

'Don't you really want to know about me and John?' The snarled question seemed to echo round the high roofed studio.

Harriet sipped from her coffee mug. 'The way you asked that question told me all I need to know,' she said gently. 'Now, schooldays first . . .'

When Harriet suggested that they go to the pub on the corner for a quick lunch, Rue blinked. Only when she checked her watch did she realise that the two of them had been talking for nearly three hours. They'd talked as much about Harriet's life as her own, and Rue found herself very much liking her earthy comments on famous people she'd met. They'd gone through the case of clothes Rue had brought, and Harriet wasn't very impressed by any of them.

'I've got to paint that hair,' she muttered, holding up one of Rue's blouses with disdain. 'And this pattern would only spoil it.'

Sitting in the pub, where Harriet was obviously already well known, Rue realised she hadn't thought of John for quite a while, the longest he'd been out of her thoughts since they parted.

'You're thinking of John Grey aren't you?' Harriet barked across the table.

Rue looked at her amazed. 'How did you know that?'

'Faces are my trade, girl. Often I can feel what people are thinking when they don't know themselves. Want to talk about him?'

'No. Perhaps later. Have you decided how you want to paint me yet Harriet?'

'All right, we'll change the subject. No, I'm still not quite sure. But I've got to have that hair.'

Normally Rue never drank at lunchtime. But Harriet had ordered a pint of bitter with her ham roll, so Rue had asked for red wine. It came in an unusually generous glass, and after Harriet had fetched another two drinks, Rue felt just vaguely uninhibited.

'Last week John Grey came into my greenhouse when I wasn't expecting him,' she told Harriet. 'It was hot and I was stripped to the waist.'

'Lucky for John Grey.'

'I could tell he . . . admired me. Harriet, would you like to paint me in the nude?'

There was a bang as Harriet thumped her glass back on the table. 'You want to get your own back,' she breathed, 'and what a lovely way to do it. That figure, that skin, that hair . . . come on, drink up. I want to get started.'

She looked at the light flush now mantling Rue's cheeks. 'Think about it as we walk back,' she advised gently, 'you don't have to. But it would be a lovely picture. And it would show him what he's missing.' She chuckled.

'Let's do it,' Rue said resolutely.

At first she was a little shy at appearing unclothed, but Harriet understood her apprehensions and soon put her at ease. Rue had to try two or three positions and then Harriet combed out her hair till it flowed down to her now naked breasts. 'Perfect,' she grunted. 'Can you hold that position?'

'I'm very comfortable,' Rue reassured her.

'Then we'll start. Talk if you want. It won't put me off.'

Rue preferred to talk than to think.

* * *

Since the Allens were doing all the work on the smallholding Rue was able to go to York every day, and by the weekend the picture was almost complete. Rue had got more and more relaxed in Harriet's company, and come very much to like the older woman's sardonic view of life. Unusually, on the Friday afternoon she referred to John.

'Has that John Grey been in touch?' she asked abruptly.

'No, and he won't be. There's no reason for him to.'

'Hmm. Well he's on television tomorrow night. Series called *A Man and his Treasures*. Talking about his pictures. I helped him a bit with it, so I'll be watching.'

'I'll watch if I have time,' Rue lied, knowing nothing would drag her away from that screen.

'Hmm. Well come and look at the latest picture he's going to add to his collection. It'll need varnishing — but this is what he's getting.'

So far Rue had deliberately avoided

looking at her picture, she wanted to see it when it was fully finished. Now she looked. Without false modesty she knew that her body was beautiful and Harriet had arranged her cascading hair to full advantage. But she couldn't quite fathom the expression Harriet had caught on her face. There was the beginnings of a smile there, and an abundance of meaning — but meaning what?

'Harriet, what's this expression on my face?' she questioned, feeling slightly troubled.

'It's the expression I saw,' Harriet answered, enigmatically, and wouldn't be drawn further.

A Man and his Treasures was on at half past nine on Saturday night. For some reason she couldn't explain to herself Rue had a bath before settling down to watch, her supper on a tray by her side.

There was the well-known introductory music of the *Arrival of the Queen of Sheba*, the aerial shots of stately homes and then the cameras cut to the programme's presenter. He said a few deferential words about Industry and Commerce playing their part in Arts Patronage, and then the camera swung to John.

Rue gasped, she couldn't help it. For the last six days the man had been almost constantly in her mind and yet she realised she had partly forgotten him. To see him talking, walking, smiling at the screen gave her a sense of loss so great that tears once again leaped to her eyes and she gripped the sides of her chair till her knuckles were white.

He was a very good television performer. He wasn't nervous and his words seemed addressed directly at her. When he smiled she felt almost compelled to smile back. In spite of her fascination with the man, she soon become engrossed with what he was saying, about his love for art and his belief that it should be much more available to the public.

'Art galleries aren't the answer,' he was explaining to the presenter. 'I believe that most paintings were intended to be hung in a room that is lived in, and this is where they are seen to best advantage.'

'But your paintings are kept in your private gallery,' the presenter said, slightly sarcastically.

'At present. They will be moved in time.'

'You aren't married Mr Grey. Will you leave the paintings to the nation, or do you in time expect to have children of your own to inherit?'

Rue caught her breath. What would John answer?

'Who can tell what will happen in the future? If I have children I'll try to bring them up to share.'

Her held breath sighed out. He had chosen not to answer the question. Then she grimaced. What did it matter to her? If he did have children — she wouldn't be the mother.

175

On Monday morning, not without some relief, she started work again on the smallholding. When she returned from her rounds of the hotels, there was a thick envelope waiting for her from the solicitors retained by her uncle. She sighed and tore it open. In effect it told her that she would have to leave but that they'd been offered a very generous settlement if she got out as quickly as possible. They recommended that she accept. Dropping the letter on the coffee table, Rue stared blankly in front of her. She hated herself for having to admit it, but she had had just the faintest hope that John might cancel the take-over of her land. He hadn't.

There was now an odd solace in her complete lack of hope and she began to plan what she could take and what she would have to leave. Even five minutes' thought showed her that the task would be monumental.

Just when Rue had forced herself to start serious planning the phone rang again. She looked at it morosely but knew she'd have to answer.

'Miss Morgan of Bagot's End?'

'That's me,' Rue said curiously. She didn't recognise the voice. It was female, obviously well-educated, and something in it suggested that the speaker was old. For all that there was a cheerfulness that she warmed to.

'My name's Lady de Fearn, of the Dower House, Wenton.'

Rue couldn't help herself. 'Honestly?' she asked.

The voice at the other end of the line giggled. 'Sounds posh doesn't it? I always enjoy it when I can say it out loud. Yes dear, it really is my name. Actually I'm the Dowager Lady de Fearn, but I think there's a limit to most things, and that passes it.'

Rue grinned into the phone. 'How can I help you, Dowager lady?'

'You can start by not ringing off till

you've heard what I've got to say. Promise?'

'Okay,' Rue said, curiously.

'Good. I own Bagot's End. I'm the woman who's going to profit by you being thrown out of your home.'

Rue's stomach twisted at this unexpected and unwanted information. 'How nice for you,' she muttered bitterly.

'It isn't very nice at all.'

'But I thought . . . some kind of an off-shore company owned it.' She forced herself to say the name. 'Doesn't John Grey administer the estate?'

'He administers all right, but I own the land. Don't ask me the details, I'm very happy to leave them all to John. But I do feel guilty about you.'

'Your feelings do you credit,' Rue said coolly. 'I don't suppose you've changed your mind.'

'If you pay for the best advice you take it. I'd no more argue with John Grey's financial decisions than I would with my doctor if he said I had cancer.

Young lady, I'd like you to come and see me.'

'I don't see much point. I don't think anything you could say would be of much interest to me.'

'Since you don't know what it is, you can't possibly judge,' the voice rapped out. 'What about four tomorrow? We'll have some tea.'

Rue hesitated. But what had she got to lose? Some remote recess of her mind taunted her with the idea that if she went it would only be to talk more about John Grey, and she shuddered at the thought. 'I'll come at four tomorrow,' she said.

'Good girl. The Dower House, Wenton. Can you find it?'

'I'll be there.' Rue rang off.

7

The first part of the journey to the Dower House at Wenton followed the road Rue had taken — was it only a fortnight ago? — to the Masked Ball at Wenton Hall. It had been the most eventful fourteen days of her life. There had been an upheaval in her ordinary, placid existence. She had lost her home and living, rescued Fiona, sneaked into the Masked Ball, met John, felt the pleasure and pain of the trip to London, been painted by Harriet. She wondered what shocks life might bring this afternoon. With a person named the Dowager Lady Millicent de Fearn she guessed that anything might happen. Whatever . . . she couldn't stop the pain of thinking about John. Rue's mood reverted to its customary bleakness.

Her little van chugged nearly to the

front gates of Wenton Hall. Then the road turned to the right, and for ten minutes followed the high grey wall of the estate. Eventually it ended in the tiny village of Wenton, all owned, Rue had discovered, by Lord Wenton himself.

Looking out over the far end of the village was the Dower House. Rue pulled in under a great tree on the edge of the village green and checked her watch; she was a quarter of an hour early. It would be ill-mannered to arrive too soon so she decided to wait a while. Steadfastly she stared at the neat grey building.

Like Wenton Hall it was Georgian, but it was much smaller, a light blue front door with just one multi-paned window on each side of it and then the estate walls. Rue pursed her lips as she looked at the front garden; it was well-laid out but it needed attention. It was a pity to spoil the overall effect when a little care would improve things.

As she watched a small black car, looking like something Noddy might drive, rattled cautiously down the road and parked in front of the Dower House. Rue stared. It was an Austin A30, a car long out of production. She vaguely remembered seeing them in her youth. Quickly she worked out its age from the number plate — it was about twenty-five years old. A white-haired woman jumped out of the driving seat and ran smartly up the drive. Rue recognised her at once, by her movements rather than her face. She was the old lady who had danced so enthusiastically at the Masked Ball. Of course, Rue sighed to herself. Charlie, the broad shouldered man she had danced with first had referred to his Mother, and he was Lord Wenton. Where else would his mother live but in the Dower House?

Where did John Grey fit in? The thought seared through Rue's mind. I must stop thinking about him she said angrily to herself, but knew it would take much more time before she could. Angrily she started the van and drove to park just behind the old black car.

* * *

'Lady de Fearn? I'm Rue Morgan.'

'Thought it was you parked under the tree there. Come on in girl. I'm just making some tea.' Rue followed the upright back of the old lady down a white-panelled passage and into a serene yellow living room, at once elegant and comfortable. 'Go and sit on the terrace. It's warm enough to be out of doors.' With a gesture towards the French windows at the end of the room, her hostess disappeared.

Rue walked slowly down the room. She liked other people's houses, she thought they revealed character. She noted the obviously well-read books and the great pile of records by the unobtrusive hi-fi system. The walls were covered in pictures, some paintings, some . . . she glanced at

183

one, blinked, looked again and then stared, entranced.

It was an old photograph, framed. Partly it had faded, but there was still a clear picture of a girl on stage, holding the hem of her long dress, and smiling as she executed a perfect high kick. There was enjoyment, exhilaration in every line of her body. Rue looked at the great mass of curls round a perfect heart-shaped face. It wasn't . . .

'Sixty years ago men came from all over England to watch me showing my knickers like that.' The humorous voice came from behind her. Rue turned, a little bewildered, to see her hostess carrying a large silver tray.

'You were a dancer?' she gasped.

'One of the best in the chorus line. It's where my husband first saw me. I can still do most of a high kick — and the splits.'

'So *that's* why you danced so well.'

'Where have you seen me dance?'

For a moment Rue wondered what to say and then decided to tell the

184

blatant truth. 'I was at the Masked Ball a fortnight ago. I was a sort of — gatecrasher.'

'If you gatecrashed that dance you must be smart. Come on let's drink some tea. I've just been for a walk along the coast and I'm parched.' She led the way through the French windows and set the tray down on a metal table in the middle of a small terrace.

At the back of the house there was first of all a small formal garden, the usual square of lawn surrounded by flower beds and a rockery. A path led through the garden to a high wall which ran for about a hundred yards parallel to the house. It was built of old red brick — a change from the customary grey stone. In the wall was a door.

'I'll pour the tea. I can tell you're curious, so why don't you nip down the path and have a look through the door. Then come back and we can have a talk.'

Rue turned to face the old lady. 'You

know, I've got a feeling I'm being set up for something,' she grinned.

Lady de Fearn beamed at her, the sweetness of the smile only emphasising the shrewdness of the eyes. 'Of course you are my dear. I'm trying to get what I want, as I usually do. Now go for a quick look and I'll pour.'

With a last thoughtful glance, Rue set off down the path.

The old wooden door creaked a little as she pushed at it. She stepped inside and gasped. As she had half guessed, through the door was an old kitchen garden. About an acre of land was surrounded in a great square by the high brick wall. On the south facing sunny side there was a long line of greenhouses, many with missing panes. Espaliered fruit bushes lined another wall. Although it seemed that someone had tried to keep order, the carefully laid out beds showed signs of neglect, and most had become entirely overgrown.

'Come and get your tea!' The voice

echoed down to her. Rue sighed, shut the door and walked back.

It was a traditional afternoon tea, with silver tea set, fine china cups and dainty sandwiches. It seemed to suit Lady de Fearn's character, even though she was currently dressed in anorak, slacks and walking boots. The tea was Earl Grey, and very strong.

'What can I do for you, Lady de Fearn?' Rue asked quietly. Suddenly she felt tired. There had been too many shocks over the past fortnight, and she suspected that this meeting was going to lead to another. She remembered the peace — boring though it might have been — of her life before she'd come to this place, and she rather regretted it had gone.

'You can listen for a minute. I'm going to give you a family history lesson — it'll perhaps explain one or two things.'

'Like losing my home and my living?' Rue put in nastily.

'Especially those two things. Now

just sit and listen before you judge, young lady!' Rue blinked and nodded.

'I'm the Dowager Lady de Fearn. Bobby, my husband, bless him, died twenty five years ago. Two days before he died he gave me that car outside as a birthday present; I'll not part with it while there's a mechanic who can keep it going.' Lady de Fearn sighed. 'Anyway, we had one son, Charlie, he's the present Lord Wenton. We also brought up the man you know as John Grey — he's actually Bobby's younger brother's child. Both his parents were killed in a nasty bit of nonsense in Africa.'

Rue's heart thudded hard against her chest. 'So . . . John is your nephew — and an orphan,' she muttered.

'That's right. He lived with us as Charlie's brother. We loved him — we still do, he can be a loveable man. But he took his parents' death hard, and I suspect he never quite got over it.' Lady de Fearn put down her cup and looked at Rue speculatively. 'Are you interested in him apart from his being the man who is throwing you out?'

'I've met him that's all,' Rue said briefly. 'Please go on.'

'The two boys were, are, completely different. Charlie loves farming. He's perfectly happy to look after the estate, his crops and animals. But something else drove John. He went to University and read economics, got a job as a financial journalist in London, and before we knew it, there he was earning millions in the City. We were so proud of him.'

Rue remembered her trip to the Hood's Bay Restaurant. 'So how come he has so many business interests up here?'

'Ah. About six years ago we had to have the roof of the Hall fixed. We had the dreaded death watch beetle. And when the estimate came in, Charlie knew we just couldn't pay it. The only thing to do was to sell the Hall. Actually, Charlie would much rather live in one of his farms, but he felt he ought to keep the building in the family as long as he could. We had a family conference. Charlie didn't want to ask John's advice, he felt it would put him under an obligation. But I said that John would be justifiably angry if he wasn't asked. So we asked him. He looked at the books, looked at the assets, got all sorts of clever little men from London to come and pry round. They got poor old Charlie quite confused. After a month he came to us with a proposition. Charlie was to handle all the farming. And John would set up a trust to handle the rest of the estate — there's all sorts of fiddly bits in it like yours. The money from the trust would keep the house maintained. The only thing he asked was that he ran it his way — and we were happy to agree.'

For almost a minute Rue sat, her head spinning, trying to make sense of all this new information.

'What sort of business man is he?' she asked eventually. 'How do the local people take to his City slicker ways?'

'Most of them like it,' came the prompt reply. 'He's seen as being firm but fair. And quite a lot of people have benefited.'

'So how did you learn about me?'

Lady de Fearn looked at her curiously. 'I'm not quite sure. I had a letter from a solicitor, setting out the situation and asking me was I entirely happy. I've no idea how he got my address.'

Rue smiled to herself secretly. She guessed her uncle had something to do with it. 'So what did you do? What was John's advice on this tricky point?'

'Young lady, I may be old but I am not senile. John looks after some of my affairs, I look after the rest. I didn't bother to ask him. What did you think of the kitchen garden?'

Rue's head whirled at the sudden change in topic. 'It once was lovely. It's sad to see it in its present state.'

'I quite agree. I had a gardener who used to live over the garage, but as he got old the work got too much for him.'

There was a pause and Lady de Fearn said casually, 'How would you like to be my new gardener?'

* * *

It took quite some time before Rue realised that this was an entirely genuine offer, and even more time before all the ramifications could sink in. Ideas, arguments, hopes and fears flashed through her mind. Eventually she was able to reply.

'My experience of doing business with your family hasn't been exactly happy so far.'

'Get yourself a solicitor like me,' was the imperturbable reply. 'If we can agree on the general conditions, then they can sort out the grubby details between them.'

'But I'm not sure I want to work for anyone else. I like being my own boss. Besides, where would I live?'

'You can have the flat over the garage that old Parker had. It's small, but it's clean and handy. As for being your own boss, I was going to say that so long as you kept my bit of garden tidy, and provided me with all the stuff I wanted, then you could still sell the rest. You're not too far away from your markets.'

'Why should you do this for me?'

Lady de Fearn snorted. 'I'm not doing this for you, I'm doing it for myself. It's impossible to get a good gardener these days, and I don't intend to pay you very much.'

'I'd need to look round,' Rue said hesitantly, 'There might be quite a lot of structural work needs doing.'

'I'll have glass put in the greenhouses, and anything else like that that needs doing. Now why don't you wander off into the garden and see what you think?'

Rue gulped. Half an hour ago she'd been hoping for a return to a quiet life. Now it looked as if even more trauma was coming her way. But at the same time she knew that this was an offer that would never be repeated. And she'd fallen in love with that walled garden. She stood. 'I'll just go and look round,' she muttered, and then sat heavily again. 'I'm afraid there's one thing we have to get sorted first. I don't want anything to do with John Grey.'

The old woman looked at her assessingly. 'Because of the way he's treated you over your land?'

Rue had to force the words out. 'No. I have met him. My dislike is . . . personal.'

Lady de Fearn smiled merrily. 'When I first came to Wenton Hall, Bobby's Grandmother was still alive. She lived here in fact. She gave me one piece of good advice about housekeeping and she remembered when they had over fifty servants. 'Millicent', she said, 'Don't ever let your family, friends or guests interfere with the servants. You've plenty of family and you can always replace friends and guests. But a good butler is worth rubies.' Well, butlers have now disappeared and there aren't too many gardeners left. Don't worry my dear. You'll never have to meet John. Unless, of course, you want to.'

'I won't ever want to meet him!'

'Of course not,' came the calm reply.

★ ★ ★

' . . . so I guess I'll take the job. The flat is very nice and I'd really like to get my hands on that garden.' Rue had driven away from the Dower House her head spinning, and driven straight to her uncle. As she told the story she still had difficulty in believing it.

'You'll want my solicitor to check everything?'

'Oh yes. Forwards, backwards and sideways. And thanks too for getting the letter to her. That was really clever.'

Her uncle smiled. 'I've still got a few friends left.'

Tom's solicitors only took three days to vet the agreement with Lady de

Fearn's solicitors and Rue then started the long task of uprooting a garden and replanting it fifteen miles away. Over the next four weeks she worked like a maniac. Lady de Fearn had the tiny garage flat decorated and it only took a morning to transfer her furniture. The plants were another matter. It was a case of spend a day preparing a bed in the new kitchen garden and an evening digging up and replanting. Some plants she knew just weren't worth the effort of moving, and some she decided she didn't want anyway — but there was still plenty to shift.

Rue worked like a person obsessed, putting in at least twelve hours a day and usually more. Lady de Fearn came into the walled garden late one evening just as she was wearily planting the last few seedlings by the light of a torch.

'Do you have to work this hard?' she asked abruptly.

Rue staggered to her feet. 'It's all got to be done sometime,' she forced out. 'There's not such a great shortage of time. You work as if you were driven by furies. Are you trying to get your plants into the ground, or something else out of your mind?'

Rue winced. She hadn't realised she was so transparent. 'I like the work,' she protested.

Lady de Fearn said nothing for a while, then, 'I'm having a whisky on the terrace. Come over when you want one.' Rue nodded and bent down again.

The hens were transported last. And finally she stood with Madge and Harry Allen and looked at the now derelict Bagot's End, a bigger mess than when she first moved in.

'There's five years of my life here,' she said wistfully.

'Five years of your past. You're just going to a different future.' Harry Allen didn't hold too much with sentiment.

'Do you think the builders will disturb you too much?'

This time it was Madge Allen who replied. 'We'll not mind that. We're sorry to see you go — but we won't mind the estate being here. There'll be a few more folk to talk to.'

Just for a moment Rue wondered if she had been a bit selfish in trying to hang on to her little estate; if she'd been standing in the way of some kind of progress. Certainly there were plenty of people hunting houses round about. 'What about Ollie, my owl?' she asked, looking at the great stand of trees behind her.

'The trees will stay. The builders have been and shown us plans of the estate. It'll be quite nice.'

Rue knew it was time to leave.

The second day after Rue moved into her new home she received a letter from Harriet inviting her to York. Rue decided she was entitled to a rest and drove over.

'Your picture's varnished and framed, what do you think of it?' Harriet waved at the far wall of the studio.

Rue walked to where the picture hung on the wall. It gave her an odd feeling to see herself naked, and in such a seductive pose. She still couldn't work out what the expression meant — and it was her expression. Harriet came and joined her. 'I know I painted it — but that's a fine piece of work,' she said with some satisfaction. Then she turned, and with a gesture Rue remembered so well, put her finger under Rue's chin and moved her head up. 'Your face is thinner. There's a new expression there. Have you been ill?'

'I've been working pretty hard.'

'Hmmm. I'm delivering this tomorrow. D'you want me to send any message?'

'How about 'Happy Birthday',' Rue said flatly.

That night, tired though she was, Rue couldn't sleep. She tried to pretend that it was because she wasn't yet used to her new flat, but her native honesty wouldn't let her fool herself. She was still in love with John. The frantic efforts of the past few weeks hadn't been necessary to her work — she had been trying to force John out of her mind. She hadn't succeeded. Every night, just as she thought she was about to sleep, some memory had crept back, making her heart thump and her eyes jerk open again in wakefulness. She climbed out of bed and made herself more milky cocoa, then sat huddled in her dressing gown clutching the warm mug. Today had made things worse. The bitter-sweet knowledge that tomorrow he'd have her picture was almost too painful to contemplate.

8

'Dear Rue Morgan' the letter read, 'I hope you don't mind my writing to you after so long, but life this past few weeks has been very hectic. I just want to thank you, not for giving me a lift to the airport, but for being kind and supportive and pushing me into action. Without you I would never have got to America and wouldn't be what I am now — Mrs Peter Hall. (My husband is shouting that he thinks you are marvellous.) At the time I didn't notice if you were wearing a ring, but if you're not married, let me recommend it.

Looking back I can hardly believe what a wimp I was, and I hope you don't think too little of me. I remember running down John Grey and I've since learned it wasn't fair, two or three people I've met think he's very nice. How was the Masked Ball?

We're coming over to England at Christmas to make peace with my parents. (If it's possible.) Please come and have dinner with us then and you can meet my wonderful husband.

Yours affectionately,
Fiona Hall (nee Blythe-Whitley).'

Rue looked grumpily at the letter and the photograph it contained, of an obviously ecstatic Fiona clutching the arm of a nice looking Peter. It was very pleasant to help other people to married bliss. Why couldn't she arrange just a little bliss for herself?

After a moment's thought she looked carefully at the envelope. The letter had been sent to her present address — where she'd only been for a fortnight. How had Fiona found where she lived? It struck her that the only point of contact between her and Fiona was John. He was the only way she could have got the new address. And that meant that he knew she was living with his aunt. Rue found this knowledge strangely disturbing.

Now she had settled, life was in some ways very pleasant. The kitchen garden still needed quite a bit of work, but that work was always rewarding. The shelter afforded by the high walls meant that her crops matured earlier and the great old fashioned greenhouses were a distinct improvement on the plastic ones she'd left behind.

Her work for Lady de Fearn was also a lot of fun. At College Rue had taken a great interest in the history of gardening, and now she turned out some of her old notes and drawings and suggested to Lady de Fearn that she redesign the garden so that it looked as it would have when it was first laid. She agreed and Rue started on her plans.

For all that, every now and again,

usually when Rue was least expecting it, there would come a sudden sense of misery, a feeling of lost love even though she'd never really had the love in the first place. Then tears would slide down her cheeks and Rue would brush them away and look for something physical to do to take her mind off things. Her feelings showed no sign of abating. Once, by accident, she passed Barry in the main street of the local little town. He nodded stiffly and walked on. Rue could have laughed when she thought of the difference between the feelings he had aroused in her and those aroused in her by John.

'You always work too hard. I'm going for a walk by the sea. Why don't you come with me?'

Rue looked up. The high walls of the garden had trapped the sun's heat and even though she was dressed in shorts and halter top, she felt sticky and uncomfortable. 'This has got to be done sometime, Lady de Fearn,' she pointed out.

'And that's another thing,' the old lady continued. 'I get more Lady de Fearn from you than the rest of my friends put together. You'd better call me Gay.'

'Why Gay?' Rue asked curiously. 'It's not your name.'

'Shortened form of Gaiety Girl. The boys started calling me it when they felt a bit old to call me Mum.'

Rue didn't ask who the boys were.

'Anyway, I'm setting off in fifteen minutes. If you fancy it, have a shower and meet me at the front.'

'I will,' Rue said resolutely, 'I feel like a rest.'

Gay — Rue thought it a lovely nickname — was a very competent driver. In her old car she negotiated the hills and bends with nonchalant skill and it wasn't long before they were dipping down a side road towards the sea. To Rue's surprise she turned off the road and bumped down a cart track for a hundred yards, eventually to stop under the shade of some trees.

'No one knows this parking space is here,' she said with satisfaction, 'it's where I always come. The car will be quite safe. Come on, this way and we can scramble down the cliff.'

For an hour they walked along the shore and in and out of the rocky coves. After a few minutes silence Gay started to talk about her youth, about how most — but not all — of Bobby's family had been against him marrying a chorus girl, and how they'd had to fight against the pressure. 'Funnily enough, the one most set against it was my father. He was a docker in Wearside. The only way Bobby got round him was to go to the pub with him and try and outdrink him.' Gay smiled. 'Imagine that. Some girls have duels fought over them. I was the prize in a beer-drinking match.' This time she laughed; Rue had to join in with her.

'Who won the match?' she eventually asked.

'My father of course. As Bobby said afterwards, victors have to be generous to the defeated.' Both laughed loudly at this, and an affronted gull screamed back at them.

'He was sensible, my Bobby. As he said, he knew what he wanted, and he didn't intend to let false pride get in his way.' There was a pause and Gay turned to look at Rue. 'You wouldn't be too proud would you?'

'No,' Rue said briefly and walked on.

After a few minutes of silence Gay said casually, 'If you've got any salad ready I'd like some this evening. I'm doing a dainty tea. John's staying with Charlie for a day or two and they're coming to see me.'

'John . . . Grey?' Rue forced out.

'The very same. I'm telling you 'cos I know you'd had your differences and you might want to make yourself scarce. On the other hand, you might want to come to tea with them and have some of my excellent cucumber sandwiches.'

'I think I'll give it a miss,' Rue said

tightly, 'but thanks for the invitation.'
'You can always change your mind.'

* * *

Deliberately, Rue went to her Uncle Tom's that night and stayed very late. Afterwards she felt a touch guilty, she knew that her keen-minded uncle had seen that she was preoccupied and guessed he knew the reason. However, he said nothing, which made her feel worse. Next morning was just as bad. Gay didn't say a thing about her little party, and when Rue tentatively asked her if all had gone well, airily said that the salad was fine. Rue went to her garden and started digging, viciously.

It was now high summer. The long-enriched soil in the walled garden was perfect for growing, and with the sun and the daily watering that Rue gave her plants, it sometimes seemed that no sooner had she planted a seedling than it was flourishing and ready to be cropped. It was hot work in the garden, but it was rewarding.

Then one morning dawned hotter than ever, with an ugly yellow sun that seemed much too large. There was no wind and merely to move made the beads of sweat form on Rue's brow and run down the sides of her face.

'It's too hot here, Rue. I'm going to the seaside to see if it's cooler.'

Rue brushed at her damp hair and nodded. 'I'll see you later Gay.'

'Could you pick some more beans for my tea? Those I had yesterday were superb.'

'I'll put some in your kitchen.'

She watched the old black car drive through the village and turned back to her tasks. Lethargically she moved down her neatly planted rows, dragging out the weeds that would flourish as quickly as her plants if she let them. It grew hotter. The yellow sun disappeared to be covered by thick grey-misty clouds. Rue had stopped work, but even as she sat in the shade of her little shed she could feel the uncomfortable pricking of heat all over her body.

The warm air stirred for the first time and there was a shivering among the trees in the estate. On a large leaf in front of the shed door Rue saw a giant damp patch appear. Then there was the individual tapping of great raindrops, gradually blending together to produce a noise like something tearing. Rain emptied out of the sky in one great deluge and Rue ran joyfully for her flat. She was sodden by the time she reached it.

After the initial ferocity the storm abated a little. But it still poured down relentlessly and Rue knew that these summer storms could last all day. She had a quick shower and settled down to some bookwork. Soon she was engrossed in her plans for Gay's Georgian garden, and the time passed.

Later in the afternoon Rue frowned. It was dark in the storm and she had her reading lamp on. But there was no light in Gay's kitchen window. Rue went to her bedroom window and squinted at the street outside. No car; Gay wasn't back. Rue shrugged and went back for her book. She'd probably stopped off somewhere for tea.

Half an hour later she lay the book down with a thump. Gay didn't stay out to tea; she liked it in her own home, especially with the salads Rue brought in. Throwing a coat over her head Rue dashed to the kitchen door; there were the beans she'd cut but there was no sign of Gay. Rue wondered if she was fussing over nothing. But she also knew she wouldn't stop.

After another half hour Rue was seriously worried. She knew Gay to be decidedly independent, she wouldn't take kindly to Rue — for example — phoning the police if there was no reason for it. But she was also eighty-five and it wasn't like her to be away for so long. Rue dashed again across to the house; still no Gay. For perhaps a minute Rue stood silently, knowing what she had to do, and yet not wanting to start a chain of events that might have unforeseeable consequences. Then she picked up the phone.

'Wenton Hall. John Grey speaking.'

It just had to be him. Rue had thought she might get through to Charlie, or perhaps a servant, but John had answered the phone and now there was no going back. For a fleeting moment Rue wondered if she was pleased or sorry.

'Hello? Who is calling please?' Rue couldn't define the effect that well-remembered voice was having on her, but it was certainly powerful.

'Hello John. It's Rue Morgan. I wonder can you tell me, is Gay . . . that is, is Lady de Fearn there?'

This time it was Rue who had to wait for an answer. The voice that eventually replied seemed untypically uncertain, as if not sure how to answer. 'Rue . . . it's nice to hear from you. Er . . . I don't think Gay is here.'

Rue gabbled. 'I'm at the Dower House. Gay went out this morning before the storm broke, saying she was going for a walk on the shore. And she hasn't come back yet, and that's not like her. I just wondered if she was at the Hall.'

This time the voice was taut and incisive. 'I'm pretty sure she's not here but I'll check. Wait there, I'm coming round.'

'But John I . . . ' Too late; he'd rung off.

For a quarter of an hour Rue paced up and down the yellow living room, wondering whether the turmoil in her mind was caused by Gay being missing or John about to arrive or a combination of both. Then there was the sound of a car drawing up outside and then an urgent knocking on the door.

'John.' She could only say one word. He stood in the vestibule, ignoring the rain that dripped from his shiny green anorak, those well remembered eyes staring at her as if to pass a message that he wouldn't or couldn't speak. Rue stared back unsmilingly. The silence seemed to drag on and on but then she remembered the real cause of his coming and managed to ask, 'You've not found her then?'

That moment of silent affinity was at an end. 'No. She's not at the Hall, I made a couple of phone calls, no one has seen her. If the car had broken down she would have phoned the garage. It looks as if she might be missing.' Even though he was speaking in the curt efficient manner he used for business there was worry in his eyes. She could tell he was concerned. He obviously loved the old lady and this made Rue love him even more.

Hesitantly Rue said, 'She said she was going to walk on the shore. I know where she usually leaves her car.'

From under his anorak he produced his portable phone, and tapped it for a moment indecisively. Then he thrust it back in his pocket. 'It's possible that she's sheltering somewhere, and I don't want to cause unnecessary alarm. We'll go and see if her car's still there.'

'I'll get my boots and coat,' Rue said.

John had borrowed a Land-Rover from the estate and the still unrelenting rain rattled on the metal roof making conversation difficult. Rue didn't want to talk. She was quite happy to sit watching the tight-lipped face of the man next to her. Expertly he drove across the drenched moors and eventually they slid off the side road and along the cart track, now a great stretch of mud.

'There's the car,' Rue cried, and the Land-Rover pulled up alongside it. There was something forlorn about the dumpy little vehicle, hidden under the great dripping trees. And it was obviously empty. John and Rue prowled round it but there was no sign as to where Gay might be.

Rue put her hooded head close to John's. 'She'll have gone down on to the shore for her walk,' she shouted against the hissing rain. 'Perhaps she got caught down there and is still sheltering.'

John nodded. 'We'll go and look. Which way is the path?'

Rue led the way through the bracken and down the cliff wall. The beating rain had turned the previously iron hard clay underfoot into a treacherous greasy mud. She slipped and was only saved from falling by John's quick grab. After that he held her hand firmly — for support only, Rue told herself. But he didn't let go when they were on level ground.

On the shore the rain pelted down unabated. She indicated the route she had taken with Gay only a week ago and the two bent their heads and plodded onwards. The beach was completely deserted, the grey rain clouded everything, making the lines of the cliffs and rocks dim and indistinct.

It was Rue who saw it first. There was something not quite right with the landscape, something didn't fit in. She stared more carefully at the rain-swept cliffs and saw it — a touch of pink halfway up the sloping dun coloured cliff wall.

She pulled at John's hand and pointed. He squinted into the rain, then ran and cautiously climbed upwards. Rue followed him, testing each precarious foothold. Gay lay in a great crack in the mud cliff, only the pink sleeve of her coat visible from below.

John dropped in beside her and felt for her pulse. From above Rue saw the white lips smile and the eyes flicker open. 'Is anything broken?' John asked urgently, and had to stoop to hear the whispered reply. He pulled off his anorak and wrapped it round the frail figure, then took out his portable phone. Rue saw the finger stab three times and realised he was ringing 999. After a terse conversation he pocketed the phone and then bent and carefully picked Gay up in his arms. Although Gay was very light, Rue marvelled at the strength that could so easily pick up a recumbent body.

With Rue steadying him John carefully slid down the muddy cliff, clutching Gay tightly. Then he set off walking across the sands towards the cars. 'The ambulance will meet us on the road,' he explained to Rue. 'I'm pretty sure she's suffering from exposure, so every minute counts.'

'Can you manage to carry her that far?' Rue asked, marvelling.

'I'll have to.' After a pause he said, 'She means a lot to me.'

'She means a lot to me too,' Rue said quietly. He looked at her briefly, nodded but said nothing.

Climbing back up the greasy cliff path was difficult. Several times John only stayed on his feet because Rue grabbed an arm and pulled him upright. But eventually they reached the top and could see the two cars ahead. John stopped, his chest heaving and sweat mixing with the rain trickling down his face. 'I need a quick rest,' he panted.

'You run on to the road and flag down the ambulance if you see it.'

Rue ran off at once. It was a mistake. After twenty yards her feet skidded from under her and she fell flat in a puddle, liquid mud splashing into her face and hair, and somehow down inside her slacks.

'Rue! Are you all right?' came a concerned bellow from behind her, but, although she was badly winded she simply climbed back to her feet, waved, and plodded onwards with a little more care. As she staggered out of the gate she saw the white and blue ambulance ahead.

The calmness and efficiency of the ambulance crew reassured her. In no time they had Gay lying covered on a stretcher; they gave her a lightning check and then one of them radioed the local hospital to say they were on their way. At their suggestion John followed in the Land-Rover while Rue rode in the ambulance and held Gay's cold hand. As the ambulance braked and then reversed towards the accident unit Rue got a shock. Gay opened her eyes, winked at her and then closed them again.

Once inside the hospital Gay was whisked off into an emergency room and Rue and John were courteously asked to wait. They gave Gay's details to the clerk and then sat in the waiting room and drank tea out of plastic cups. After a while Rue became aware that she was wet through and uncomfortable. She shivered and John turned to her solicitously. 'Rue, I'd forgotten, you had that fall. How d'you feel? Shall I get you a taxi home so you can change?'

'I'm all right,' Rue growled. 'And I want to wait to see if Gay's all right.' John's hand patted hers, then gripped it. Rue found it comforting and squeezed back.

'Friends of Lady de Fearn? Would you like to come this way?' What seemed to Rue like a ludicrously young doctor led them through the waiting room and into a little office. 'We've given her a thorough examination and there doesn't appear to be anything organically wrong. Nothing is broken. Of course, if you're eighty-five any accident is risky, so we'll keep her in for a couple of days' observation.'

'She's going to be all right?' Rue asked.

'No reason at all why not. I hope I'm in as good shape when I'm her age.'

'Can we see her?'

'She's sleeping for the moment, but you can look in.' The doctor looked hard at the pair of them. 'Here's a piece of free medical advice. You both should go home, have a bath and get warm. There's nothing you can do here.'

As he spoke Rue realised she was cold, tired, dirty and wet-through. A bath sounded like Heaven.

John was speaking to the doctor. 'You'll let us know if there's any change in her condition?'

'Of course. We have your phone number.'

'Then we'll go. Oh, and Doctor — thank you.'

A nurse led them to a tiny ward where Gay was sleeping, the colour already coming back into her cheeks. Then John led her out to the Land-Rover and drove her home.

'How d'you feel?' he asked after a few moments silence.

Rue considered his question. 'I'm relieved that she's going to be all right. Other than that I feel terrible, and I think I'm going to cry.' He put his arm round her and she leaned on his wet shoulder and sobbed.

John drove her to the Dower House and bundled her upstairs. 'Get those clothes off and have a long bath. I'll leave a dressing gown outside for you. I'm going to the Hall to talk to Charlie and then I'll come back here and get us something to eat.'

'But I live next door over the garage,' Rue protested. 'I'll be all right there.'

'Just for once do as you're told. Stay in that bath for half an hour.'

Rue didn't feel up to arguing. Painfully she peeled off her wet and mud-stained clothes while the bath filled. Then she tossed in a generous handful of Gay's expensive bath salts and lowered herself in the scented water. It stung as it reached her waist; looking down she realised that the fall on the path had been harder than she thought, there was a great graze and an ominous bruised feeling to her ribs. However, the pain went as she luxuriated there. For ten minutes she lay there doing nothing, the water lapping under her chin, then she sat upright and shampooed the dirt out of her hair. Then another long calming rest . . .

'Have you gone to sleep in there?' There was a rattle at the door and John's cheerful voice shouted at her.

'Just coming,' she called, and cast an apprehensive glance at the bathroom door which she had forgotten to lock.

'Shall I bring you in a cup of tea?'

'You will *not!*' Rue heard his laughter

as he walked down the stairs.

She gave her hair a final rinse, tied it up in a towel, then dried herself and cautiously picked up the dressing gown from outside. It was an exquisite red silk robe, obviously very old. She wondered if Gay had worn it when she was still a dancer, it made her feel pampered and luxurious. At the top of the stairs she stopped. For the past few hours she and John had been united in their worry for Gay; nothing else had seemed important. But now Gay was as well as could be expected, she wasn't a problem. And Rue was walking, half naked, down to a man whom she loved, and yet had rejected and tried to forget. It wasn't going to be easy.

John was waiting for her at the bottom of the stairs. In the few minutes he'd been away he'd managed to change, Rue thought the white shirt and black sweater suited him. She looked down apprehensively.

'I've seen Charlie and he's gone to

the hospital. He'll phone us later. And I grabbed a few provisions out of the kitchen.'

'I'm hungry,' Rue said, then sense and resolution grabbed her. 'Look John, I want to go home.'

'Do you want to or do you think you ought to? There is a difference.'

'I know the difference! All right, I think I ought to.'

'We've both had a rough afternoon and I'm as hungry as you are. Look, if there's any talking to be done between us, let's leave it until we've eaten — until tomorrow morning even.' She flinched at the idea of talking. The last time they'd met she'd said nearly everything, and she couldn't see John forgetting that easily. However . . . 'Yes, all right,' she said.

'Then come down and eat.'

The few provisions he claimed he'd grabbed turned out to be a minor feast. There were two kinds of cheese, a cold roast chicken, fresh rolls and a tossed salad in a large plastic container. From the kitchen came the savoury smell of a game pie warming in the oven. The two sat by the fire which had been laid but not lit and John flicked a match into it. Then, as Rue gazed at the growing flames, he walked to the fridge, and shortly afterwards she heard a satisfying pop. He returned with two filled flute glasses and the champagne wrapped in a damp towel.

'What shall we drink to Rue?'

'We'll drink to Gay's recovery,' she said quickly.

'What else?' The way he said it suggested he had something in mind and she could see a great yearning in his eyes. She felt her cheeks go pink as she clinked glasses and then sipped daintily from her champagne.

For ten minutes they ate and drank in companionable silence, Rue sitting in Gay's armchair, John sprawled out at her feet. She felt her great fatigue gradually lifting, but as it did she realised that there were more problems to come. Why worry? She held out her glass to be refilled. A little later she was surprised to hear a second pop.

'Are you opening another bottle?' she asked, surprised.

'It's necessary. You've just emptied the first.'

'Wooops.' Rue decided to slow down a little. Relief after excitement, the hot bath, the food and the excellent champagne all conspired to bring about a feeling of contentment. 'How did you like your birthday present?' she asked, and then blushed scarlet at her own boldness.

'I thought it was magnificent,' he said softly. 'It's the centrepiece of my collection. There's only one thing I want more . . . '

'What's that?' she questioned curiously.

'It's only a copy. I want the original.'

'But . . . ' She worked out what he meant, and said nothing.

For some time now his hand had been playing with her bare foot, stroking her toes and gently caressing the sensitive skin of her instep. Now he stretched up a hand to hers, and eased her down to the rug beside him. It seemed the most natural thing in the world for him to slip an arm round her back to support her, and then to pull her to him. It was a long and gentle kiss but when he broke away his chest was heaving and Rue could feel her own pulse begin to race. To hide her emotion she picked up her glass and sipped.

'Whose idea was it to paint you like that?'

'Mine,' Rue said simply, 'I wanted you to know what you were missing.'

'I knew what I was missing. And I want it more than ever.' His hand moved across her and twitched at the towel round her head. It fell away and damp hair cascaded down over her shoulders.

'Now look what you've done! It's all wet!'

'It still looks lovely. Here, lean towards me and I'll dry it.' Before she could object he had taken the towel and was rubbing her hair vigorously.

'You don't do it like that,' she yelped, 'I've got a hair dryer.'

'This gives me an excuse for getting close to you.' When he had finished he threw down the towel and smoothed her hair back. Then he grasped the sides of her face with both hands and pulled her to him again. This time his kiss was fiercer and she thrilled to the passion she knew she aroused in him.

'I've looked at that picture every night. It's been driving me mad. I know every inch of it, every touch of colour to your skin . . . and that smile!'

'I didn't know what it meant,' Rue faltered, 'Harriet just said she painted what she saw.'

'Harriet is a witch! She knew what it would do to me. But now here you are — my picture — but real.'

As he spoke his hand moved to the neck of the dressing gown. Rue knew she could stop him but she didn't want to. It seemed to her that the soft noise of the silk on her skin was the loudest thing she had ever heard, his half-felt breath being the only other thing to break the silence. His hands moved to her shoulders — and she shrugged off the dressing gown, unselfconsciously and proudly.

'Rue, I . . . ' he said hoarsely and his hands reached for her. In the hall the telephone rang.

'Damn!' he cursed. 'Rue, we'll ignore it.'

'It might be the hospital,' she pointed out. It was the right thing to say. He leaped to his feet.

'Charlie?' she heard him say, and a moment later he shouted to her through the half open door. 'Charlie's at the hospital, Gay's all right.' John had suggested that they get a consultant to look at Gay and for a moment Rue could hear him discussing it with Charlie. She pulled the dressing gown back on her shoulders and climbed stiffly to her feet.

'Walker's the best man in Harley

Street,' she heard John say, 'I could phone him at once.'

She moved to Gay's bureau where she knew there was a pen and note pad.

When John returned the living room was empty. The remains of their supper, two Champagne bottles, one half full and on the coffee table a single sheet of paper. He glanced at the French windows at the end of the room and then picked up the note.

'Thanks for the supper,' he read. 'Forgive me, but for this reason and that I'm not staying tonight. Will you pick me up tomorrow morning and take me to see Gay?' The rest of the sheet was more or less bare, but near the bottom there was a tiny postcript. 'I think I love you. Rue.'

He thrust the paper into his pocket and poured the rest of the champagne into his glass. He sipped, and after a while he smiled.

* * *

As if to make up for the storm, the next day was gloriously sunny. Rue was up early and picked a bouquet of flowers to take to the hospital. It was Sunday and she could hear the sound of church bells rolling in from the next village. John hadn't set a time for calling, but she guessed he'd arrive about ten.

In fact his car — his Jaguar this time she noted — drew up at half past nine. A little apprehensively she scurried down the steps to meet him. He looked at her without smiling. 'Did you sleep well?'

'Perfectly, thank you,' she answered demurely. 'In fact better than I have in weeks. How about you?'

· 'No. I had things on my mind — but you'd know about that.' Suddenly he smiled, and Rue felt weak-kneed at the sight of him. 'I've had a message from the hospital — will you get a few things to take in to Gay, she says you'll know the kind of thing she wants. And while you're getting them, can I have a coffee?'

'Come on in.' Rue ushered him into her tiny living room and then went across to the Dower House to pick up nightie, dressing gown and some clothes for when Gay might be ready to come home. She noticed, with just a touch of guilt, that all evidence of last night had disappeared. The towels were in the dirty linen basket, the plates and glasses had been washed. But it did happen, she thought to herself, and smiled.

As if by mutual consent they didn't talk much as they drove to the hospital, but the silence was an amiable one. On the cassette player was Rue's favourite *Songs for Swinging Lovers*.

'Do you like Sinatra?' she asked, curiously.

'You do. I saw it in your bungalow. So I bought it — and I've come to like it.' He turned and winked at her. 'And I want to be a swinging lover.'

'Time will tell.'

In the hospital they were shown straight to Gay's small ward. The old lady looked well as they both kissed her.

'The eggs here are terrible,' she said as soon as they sat down, 'not half as good as yours, Rue.'

'Other than that, how are they looking after you?' John put in.

'Very well indeed. I haven't been in hospital since I had Charlie — and I'm agreeably surprised.'

As Rue showed Gay the contents of her bag and was asking if there was anything more she should bring, a nurse flitted in and whispered that someone would like a word with John. Rue and Gay chatted idly about the garden for ten minutes and then John returned. From his irate expression Rue could tell that something was wrong. He was angry, and yet there was just a touch of grudging humour in his eyes.

'I've just had a word with the consultant,' he said without preamble. 'He wanted to know if you were over-imaginative or hysterical at all.'

'I hope you told him I most certainly am not,' Gay snarled.

'I did. He said in that case, you were faking. There was no reason why you couldn't have walked up to your car and driven home.'

'What a thing to say about your dear old Aunt,' Gay murmured, with obvious relish.

'You've wasted hospital time!'

'I'll send them a large donation,' came the imperturbable answer.

'But why did you do it Gay?' Rue cried out. 'Didn't you know we would all worry about you?'

'I'm an old harridan my dear, and I interfered secure in the knowledge that my great age would save me from reproach.'

'Interfered in what?'

'John told me he'd given you a crystal slipper — you're a real Cinderella. Well I decided to be the Fairy Godmother — it's brought you two together hasn't it? I told you once I liked my own way.'

'You're a wicked old woman,' John roared.

'I am aren't I?' came the complacent reply. 'Now you two had better go and let me get some sleep.' With complete determination she slid down the bed and pulled the blankets up to her chin. 'Oh by the way,' her muffled voice continued, 'my car keys are there. Pick it up and take it home will you?'

'I need strength,' Rue heard John mutter, but he did pick up the keys.

★ ★ ★

The cart track was still damp, but not the morass it had been yesterday. Rue and John walked to the little black car and Rue realised that she'd have to drive it back, they'd be separated. 'Can we go for a walk for a few minutes?' she asked.

'I'd like that.' Once again they slid down on to the deserted shore, but this time the sun was shining, and the gently moving sea beat onto bright golden sand.

For a moment or two Rue walked in silence, her head bent, and then she reached out and grasped John's hand. 'There's things I've got to tell you.' They paced onwards, John realising that Rue didn't want any comment yet. 'I was an only child and my father brought me up. My mother died having me. He was a quiet, gentle man — he loved me, I was the centre of his life. Anyway, after thirty years as a clerk he was made redundant. He didn't mind too much, I was at College and he looked forward to retirement. He was given the choice — have a pension or a lump sum. A man he thought a friend told him to opt for a lump sum, he'd invest it for him. Well, my father got his lump sum, his friend invested it, lost it all and went to look for other suckers and . . . my father gassed himself.'

After a while, John asked gently, 'So you've hated anyone who had anything to do with money ever since?'

'Yes. I know it's unreasonable, I know a lot of people use money well. But it just doesn't feel that way to me.'

John put his arm round her, squeezed, but said nothing for a while. Then, 'I know why you've told me. Believe me, I sympathise and I'm sorry. Look, come back to the car now. There's something I've been meaning to show you.'

'To do with money?'

'Well, to do with my money.' He hugged her again, but would say no more.

In the back of his car was a great pile of unopened Sunday newspapers, he had obviously bought them before he picked her up that morning. Rummaging through them he found the thickest, threw aside all but the financial section and offered it to Rue. 'Look at the front page.'

She did. The headline read 'John Grey Sells Up. Biggest Shock in

Years.' Rue skimmed through the article unbelievingly. Much of the detail she just couldn't understand but the general sense appeared to be that he had stopped dealing in shares and intended to retire . . . with, the article remarked, 'A very considerable personal fortune.'

'But . . . why have you done it?'

'What you said when you left me hurt. I thought about it quite a bit, and I realised that . . . well you weren't entirely right, but you weren't entirely wrong either. So I decided to get out.'

'You did that because of what I said?'

'I did it because you said it. I thought the money had come between me and something I wanted more than money.'

Rue had difficulty in swallowing. 'You did it for me? But . . . what will you do now?'

'I'm going to show you. Drive back — not to the Dower House but to Wenton Hall. I'll follow behind you.'

Gay's old car wouldn't move fast, which was just as well. It seemed to find its own way back to the Hall, Rue was only half conscious of driving, stopping, signalling. A discreet fifty yards behind her was the Jaguar, she watched that as much as the road in front. And all the while she thought of John.

The path into the Hall was the same as it had been when last she had visited — so little time ago. She pulled up some distance from the front of the building and John drew up behind her. Parked in front of the steps was a large removal van, and men were carrying furniture into it.

'What's happening?' she asked John, who had come to stand by her side.

'Charlie's moving out. He's never liked the Hall too much, he'd rather live in a farm next to his beloved animals. Sadly, he and his wife can't have children, so there's no reason for him to stay.'

'He's not selling up?' Rue cried.

240

'That would be terrible.'

'It costs a vast amount to keep the old pile going,' John countered. 'And it's far too big for just two people.' Rue blushed a little.

They walked towards the formal gardens Rue had noticed before, they were beautiful but just a little neglected. John went on, 'He's not selling up, just moving out. And I'm moving in. I'm going to spend some of what the paper delicately called a very considerable personal fortune in renovating the building — and for that matter the grounds. Then I'm going to put my pictures in it, and I'll open it to visitors — but only when I feel like it. I don't want the Hall to make money, I want it to be lived in, to be a home for a family.'

'A family?' Rue questioned hoarsely.

'Husband, wife, three dogs, a cat, couple of horses. Children in time of course. Then we'd need a pony each for them.'

'A wife?' she croaked.

He put his arms round her, bent and kissed her. 'If you'll marry me,' he said, 'otherwise it's back to London and making yet more money.'

Rue looked up at him, tall smiling and infinitely desirable. Then her eye skimmed over the house in its setting of gardens. 'Let's go in and make some plans,' she whispered.

THE END